A CAPPELLA

Anthem Press
An imprint of Wimbledon Publishing Company
www.anthempress.com

This edition first published in UK and USA 2013
by ANTHEM PRESS
75–76 Blackfriars Road, London SE1 8HA, UK
or PO Box 9779, London SW19 7ZG, UK
and
244 Madison Ave. #116, New York, NY 10016, USA

Original title: Mubanso
Copyright © Mariko Koike 1990
Originally published in Japan by Shueisha, Tokyo
English translation copyright © Juliet W. Carpenter 2013

A CIP record for this book is available from the British Library.

ISBN-13: 978 0 85728 044 2 (Hbk)
ISBN-10: 0 85728 044 9 (Hbk)

This title is also available as an eBook.

This book has been selected by the Japanese Literature Publishing Project (JLPP),
an initiative of the Agency for Cultural Affairs of Japan.

A CAPPELLA

Mariko Koike

Translated by Juliet W. Carpenter

ANTHEM PRESS
LONDON · NEW YORK · DELHI

I dedicate this book to my friend M.I., who lived through that era with me, and to everyone else who knew me then.

PROLOGUE

When I was young, I hoped and prayed that the town I lived in would never change. Places like the old-fashioned candy store where I got stickers when I bought gum, or the bridge girder where my friends and I would sit and lick popsicles on our way back from the swimming pool. The old air raid shelter where we had adventures; the unmanned railway crossing, said to be haunted because once a year there was a fatal accident there. The abandoned factory and empty weed-grown lot where grownups said we mustn't play... if one day all of these should disappear, where would I go?, I used to wonder anxiously. Sometimes, imagining that my town had undergone drastic change, I would lie sleepless in bed and sob without knowing why.

But in the end, inevitably, the day came when I had to go away; my father's job meant that we never stayed long in one place. And over time this habit of leaving town before change set in led to a sense of immutability. I found myself really believing that places didn't change. In my heart they lived on and on, untouched by time.

Refusing to admit that things do change, clinging stubbornly to the past like a spoiled child, is sentimental and immature, I know. And yet I still have a secret feeling that the places I used to live in exist somewhere, even now, inviolate. Absurd, I admit, yet part of me wants it to be true. On nights when I'm too tired to sleep, I conjure up images from the various places where I used to live. Curiously, in my memory they are black and white. The candy store, the empty lot, the unmanned railway crossing and the dilapidated bridge over the stream come back to me in a monochrome which is somehow lacking in reality.

I give myself over to the familiar old scenes. I search for them, wanting to find them again the way they used to be, to meet my old playmates as they used to look; then smile ruefully at the silliness of what I'm doing. *How old are you?* I tell myself. *Get a grip.*

But memories, like the bits of colored glass in a kaleidoscope, shift constantly. Now lighter, now darker in tone, they tumble swiftly, moving inexorably toward a certain shape. *Stop*, I think, *you have to stop it.* And yet despite myself, the hand gripping the kaleidoscope won't drop away. Finally, as if it has been impatiently waiting its turn, the image of one place I have lived in coalesces into view. I can feel it tugging me down into the depths of consciousness.

I close my eyes and turn my face away, refusing to look...but however tightly I shut my eyes, however I twist and turn, second by second the memories revive in images of crystal clarity. I see again every detail of those painful events of twenty years ago.

In the northerly city of Sendai lived the first person I ever loved. I knew he didn't love me, but even so I loved him to distraction. Wataru Domoto. That was his name. *Wataru...* Even now, all these years later, sometimes I'm gripped by the urge to dig a hole in the ground and shout his name into it over and over like a crazy woman.

The city streets were filled with a desperate revelry. The city was overripe. Like a fruit on the point of falling from the tree, it gave off a heady, intoxicating smell.

Remembering, and unable to stop a rising tide of emotion, I lie in bed with my head in my hands and grind my teeth. Twenty long years have passed since it all happened, time I spent running away. Running and running and running, until sometimes I would feel for the space of a moment that it was finally behind me. That too was an illusion. Along with my memories of the city, what happened there is still within me, hidden away deep in the folds of my mind like a bruise that won't heal. For a number of years now, memories of those events have come back night after night to haunt me, smothering me in bitter sentiment. A sweet yet awful torture.

Just ten days ago, I decided to go back. It's absurd to be so fixated on one thing, suffering in secret like a child who wets his bed. Not like me at all. That's what I told myself.

I telephoned Wataru's parents and managed to get the name of the place where his sister, Setsuko Domoto, works. The voice on the phone was cold, but I was content just to find out that much.

I wanted to see Setsuko. Doing so would bring me some relief, I hoped. She was the one person in town who would still know me. At the thought, I was unable to restrain myself.

I boarded the bullet train in Ueno and arrived in Sendai two hours later. Two hours! That's all it took for me to reach the place I'd fled from and obsessed over for twenty years.

As I stepped out of the brand-new station building, I couldn't help laughing to myself in dismay: nothing was the same. The buildings were all new, there was a new subway line, and the wide street in front of the station was crowded with big banks, movie theaters, department stores, and other establishments I'd never seen before. The difference of twenty years was enormous. No sign of the past remained. I laughed privately again, with a wistful sigh.

It was after nine p.m. when I left my hotel on Aoba Street. The crisp smell of autumn was in the air, and the breeze felt cold against my skin. My arms, exposed in a short-sleeve linen suit jacket, were soon covered in gooseflesh – and not only because of the cool temperature. I felt extremely tense.

The Kokubunmachi area was a short walk from the hotel. In the old days, among the seedy bars, hotels with hourly rates, and cheap eating places, it had contained a scattering of ordinary coffee shops, but the neighborhood had since had a makeover: now it was a posh amusement area lined with elegant buildings.

I threaded my way through crowds of dressed-up bar hostesses and men, on the lookout for a bar called Setsuko. It wasn't easy to find. Every building glowed with bright neon signs advertising bars and clubs. The one I wanted had to be there, but the only way to find it was to stand in front of each building one by one, crane my neck, and hunt. I could have gone to a police box to find the address, or just stepped into a phone booth, dialed information for the number and called to ask for directions; but I chose not to. I wanted to locate the bar myself. I especially didn't want to call and hear Setsuko's voice come on the line. I knew that if I did, I'd only panic needlessly and end up bolting.

Finally, after wandering back and forth rubbing shoulders with people who'd had a few too many, I spotted it: a six-story building bearing the sign "Setsuko." It was slightly battered-looking, set back from the main road. Amid the garish red and yellow neon all around, the small sign gave off a cozy pale blue light, like a single modest violet in a garden of gaudy blooms.

The bar was in the basement. I took the stairs, avoiding the elevator. Right at the back was a surprisingly simple old-fashioned wooden door, the entrance to the bar. As I stood in front of it, hesitating, the door next to it swung open and out staggered a man accompanied by a hostess. From inside came the sounds of rowdy karaoke singing. The redheaded hostess looked at me curiously.

I had a sudden impulse to run back up the stairs and beat a retreat to my hotel. On the other side of this door was Setsuko. What look would cross her face when she saw me? Would she pretend not to know me, to keep from reviving unpleasant memories?

Her eyes still on me, the redheaded hostess whispered something to her drunken customer, who put his arms around her and guffawed. I looked away, and resolutely opened the door.

The interior was small and dimly lit. Beside the bar were a couple of booths. Posters for jazz concerts adorned the sooty, white-plastered walls. The only customers were two men seated at the bar; two women stood behind it. When I came in, they all turned and looked at me. I stood stock still in the entrance until I was satisfied that the older woman was indeed Setsuko Domoto.

She seemed not to recognize me, only calling out a mechanical welcome and letting her gaze slide on. She was preparing some kind of snack. A customer said something funny to her, and she tilted her head and laughed sweetly. I went over to a booth and sat down.

Some music was playing, but it made no impression on me. Holding myself erect, I looked over at the bar, where Setsuko still laughed at the customer's joke. A dark brown dress and small dangly pearl earrings. Short hair cut straight across, falling just below her ears. She was as attractive as ever. Hers was the kind of beauty that could put other women's backs up. Oh, how jealous I'd been of those eyes, that nose, that mouth! Her cameo features, so like her brother's, had been the source of such absurd misunderstanding.

The younger long-haired woman minced over to take my order. After a second's hesitation, I asked for a Coke highball. She looked down at me blankly. Aware of Setsuko's presence, I said louder, "A Coke highball, please."

Whether she had never heard of such a drink or merely wanted to make sure they had some Coke on hand, the girl looked quizzically at Setsuko behind the bar. Setsuko looked over at her, still laughing. Her eyes shifted, and she registered my presence. I met her gaze, not breathing. She stood motionless, her expression frozen.

All sounds died away. For a moment her eyes lost their sparkle, as if dead. The pretty red lips parted slightly. I tried to smile. I don't know if I succeeded.

Setsuko slowly emerged from behind the bar. The two customers went on cracking inane jokes, but she paid no attention. She came up to me and stopped, biting her lip, her long lashes fluttering, and said, "You're Kyoko, aren't you? Kyoko Noma."

I nodded dumbly, like a child. I didn't know what to say. Letting out my breath, I clenched my hands tightly under the table. "I ordered a Coke highball," I said with an awkward smile, "but maybe you don't make such an old-fashioned drink."

Looking now as if she might start crying, Setsuko smiled back at me. "Oh, yes we do. We can make as many as you want."

I nodded. "We drank a lot of them back then, didn't we? Make two, if you like. One for yourself."

Her lips quivered. She stood still for a moment, staring down at me. "How've you been?" I asked. "Is everything all right?"

She nodded. "What about you?"

I said I was fine. She nodded rapidly several times, wiped the corners of her eyes with the tips of her little fingers, and gave a cheery smile.

While she mixed the drinks, I took a cigarette out of my purse and lit it. My hands were shaking somewhat. The Rolling Stones' "As Tears Go By" started up softly.

Twenty years ago, my friend Ema used to like Mick Jagger. "Not that monkey face of his," she'd say, "but his voice and style. He's so cool – when he's middle-aged, he'll still be cool. So will Wataru and Yunosuke. They've got the same style as him, don't you think?"

I'd been unable to answer her. For some reason, I couldn't picture either Wataru or Yunosuke as middle-aged men. I knew nothing then, still contentedly ignorant. But perhaps her comment about Mick being middle-aged – and Wataru and Yunosuke, too – had set off some kind of secret warning bell.

Mick Jagger reached middle age. He still sings the same old songs in the same old way. Wataru and Yunosuke, on the other hand, only smile like statues out of photographs faded to sepia. Had they still been living in Sendai, I might have encountered them as middle-aged men. I might have seen their thinning hair, heard them speak defensively of their lives, the way men do. But the events of winter 1970 intervened, and those two youths, along with their great secret, vanished out of my life forever.

1

In my third and final year of high school, I lived with my aunt. My father had been transferred back to his company's main office in Tokyo after just a year and a half at the Sendai branch. Because of his frequent transfers, I had already changed schools six times by then: three times in elementary school, twice in junior high and once in high school.

The first character in my name is difficult for children to read and write; perhaps that's why on the first day of elementary school the teacher would invariably write out my full name on the blackboard in large characters, adding the pronunciation in smaller writing to the right. Having to stand in front of the class with my back to my name, the other kids' curious eyes trained on me, was embarrassing. Nevertheless, mindful of my mother's admonitions about good manners, I would force myself to smile brightly and say, "Hello, everyone," with an ingratiating bow of the head. I always followed this up with a witty self-introduction.

At first everyone would be nice to me, though they kept their guard up. They eyed me warily from a certain distance, like a pack of monkeys waiting for a newcomer to bare his teeth so they could turn on him in a vicious mauling.. To impress on them that I was good-natured and not stuck-up, I sometimes had to play the class clown, like the amiable, wisecracking figure in a wholesome children's story. I would tell a silly joke to make them laugh. When this didn't work, I'd go right ahead and laugh at it myself.

What's strange is that whatever school I transferred to, I always made friends. Usually they were nice kids, the kind who put up a strong front but are quick to give in. The upper echelon, those with an unspoken sense of privilege, stayed away from me; and nor did I have anything to do with the ones who were openly inferior.

After a trying three months, the class would no longer regard me as an outsider. But after six months or a year, just when the next new kids had arrived and I was starting to relax, it would again be my turn to mount the podium – this time to say goodbye. A few days later, I'd be in a classroom in some other school in some other part of Japan, standing with my back to a blackboard on which "Kyoko Noma" was written, smiling and bowing my head.

How this childhood may have affected me I can't say. The experience of repeatedly transferring to new schools toughens you, they say, but I have my doubts. It never made me any tougher or smarter; it only made me long for the day when I would be free to live apart from my parents.

My father had an exceptionally strong sense of family. He was one of those people who are convinced that children raised without both parents turn delinquent. Back in the spring of 1969, his decision to let me stay behind in Sendai was largely my aunt's doing.

Widowed at an early age, my aunt supported herself by teaching piano in a residential neighborhood of Sendai. Back then she would have been around fifty. She invariably wore a kimono, even when walking the dog or vacuuming the house, and always looked like a model for a class in the art of wearing one. When I went to visit her, she never failed to tell me that my clothes were too loud or that a high school girl had no business getting a permanent. Then she would get me to weed her garden.

She was childless and lived alone, nunlike in her life of ordered simplicity. At the time I was incapable of imagining how lonely she must have been, so when she suggested, "Kyoko, how would you like to move in with me? Then you could stay here in Sendai 'til you finish high school," I was silent. Not even the prospect of staying on in Sendai was enticement enough for me to want to live with her. Given the choice, I'd have gladly slept at the school rather than endure her complaints about my clothes and hair and spend my weekends weeding her garden.

But to my father, she was a trusted elder sister. When she came over and volunteered to take me in, in a tone that might have been either joking or serious, he surprised me by going for the idea.

"You've got no children of your own," he said. "You know, it might be just the thing."

My mother chimed in, "And after all, it's just another year 'til she graduates. She'll be thrilled. Won't you, Kyoko?"

"I'm no pushover, though," said my aunt, eyeing me sternly and affecting a gruff tone. "I won't spoil you the way your mother and father do."

"If you do take her in, you've got to lay down the law," my father agreed in all seriousness. "Look at the times we live in. Kids today – take your eyes off them and there's no telling what kind of trouble they'll get into."

The grownups agreed back and forth that high-schoolers today were a disaster. Most Sendai high schools had been affected by the strife on college campuses. My father's opinion was that every kid who put on a helmet, joined a demonstration, and threw stones at riot police should be put up against a wall and shot. My aunt told us with a worried frown that she'd seen long-haired high school students sitting in coffee shops, smoking cigarettes and reading communist books aloud to each other.

My father said casually, "Kyoko, *you* don't have any books like that, do you?"

"No," I said. "Come on, Dad. You've *seen* my bookshelf."

"Oh, right," he said, and looked away.

My parents had the impression that I wanted to live with my aunt. Outwardly I got along with her fine and had never said a word against her orderly, solitary lifestyle. My father stipulated four conditions: I was never to join a demonstration or rally; I was to gain first-round admission to a university in Tokyo and not take a year off to try again; I was not to skip classes; and I was to be home by seven every night. As long as I agreed to these conditions, he would allow me to live with her.

There was no other way for me to stay in Sendai. I did have friends who would have put me up for the coming year, but I couldn't take advantage of their hospitality knowing that it would anger my father. Besides, I liked my friends but found their families hard to take. People in the Tohoku district, when they have guests, serve crisp homemade pickles as snacks. Having to sit and listen to somebody's parents crunch loudly on pickles while they lectured me about not worrying my father was not my idea of fun.

Realizing that my only choice was to stay with my aunt, I pretended to swallow my father's conditions. Little by little, I moved my things into her place. I didn't have very much. A few favorite outfits, some pajamas and underwear, some records and books I treasured... that about did it. A young guy from my father's company brought my desk and bed over in a truck.

Once I was moved in, I spent my time ditching school to attend anti-war rallies in the park with my friends, smoke cigarettes in jazz coffee shops, and make the rounds of cheap movie theaters. I thought that living apart from my parents would bring about some sort of change in my life, but it didn't really happen.

The day before my parents left, I was elected chairman of the Committee for the Struggle to Abolish School Uniforms, a secret organization at the high school I was going to then. Almost all of the high schools in the prefecture were single-sex, public and private alike, and mine was no exception. Discontented by the placid atmosphere of an all-girls school, I'd begun to mouth rebellious opinions I'd picked up somewhere, changing before long from a quiet, ordinary transfer student into a flaming activist.

Setting up the committee had been my idea in the first place, so perhaps it was natural that I should be put in charge of it, but I felt only mounting gloom. I was well aware that someone who enjoyed being a smart aleck, arguing that black was white, was totally unfit to lead an organization. It was just that I was irked by our absurd school rules – no square-collared blouses, mandatory socks, no permanents, no hair ribbons or combs – and by the unfashionable school uniform I had to wear, shiny from over-ironing.

The rest of the positions were quickly decided. My best friend Juri became secretary. One member of the committee belonged to the hard-left Middle Core Faction, but most of us had no political experience of any kind.[1] We were just average high school kids.

[1] The *Middle Core Faction* were a large militant group that played a major role in the demonstrations of the sixties, supporting an end to the US military presence in Vietnam, among other causes.

The other girls applauded me. I went through the motions, laying out what I hoped to accomplish as chairman, and they all said "No objection."

Afterwards, Juri, Reiko and I went to our favorite ramen noodle shop. Slurping miso-flavored ramen, I muttered that I didn't really want to be chairman, and they nodded sympathetically and said they understood.

"But I got picked, so I've got to do it, huh."

"Right," said Juri. "You've got what it takes. Hang in there."

"I bet I get sick of it before we're done, though."

"Worry about that when it happens," advised Reiko. "You can always decide later what to do."

"Listen. Next all-school assembly, I'll grab the podium, okay?" said Juri. "All you've gotta do is work behind the scenes."

"That's right," said Reiko. "Leave the hairy stuff to Juri. She can handle it."

"She should be the chairman," I said sincerely. Juri was better qualified. Partly because she wore her silky hair in a mushroom cut like a member of a rock band and spoke like a boy, she radiated a kind of energy that transcended gender. She expressed her anger and frustration through quiet pressure. When a teacher she disliked gave a test, she unfailingly turned in a blank paper. When the teacher went berserk and ordered her to stand in the hallway as punishment, she would uncomplainingly oblige, standing for hours on end with her hands thrust into her pockets, an invincible smile on her face. When she challenged you on something, she did so bluntly, to your face. She never buttered anyone up, never groused, never altered herself to fit in. I liked Juri a lot, and I trusted her.

"Not me," she demurred with a short laugh. "I'm irresponsible and I've got no integrity. A leader's gotta be someone like you, Kyoko."

"I'm irresponsible, too," I replied, a little miffed. Back then people competed over something as silly as this. Being seen as a person of integrity, someone decent and fair-minded, got my back up for some reason.

"Anyway, don't sweat it," she said, slurping the broth in her bowl and blowing her nose loudly into a paper napkin. "I'm with you all the way. Let's have some fun."

After some jasmine tea we left the ramen place, went to a jazz coffee shop and smoked. Juri talked passionately about how the committee should be run, and Reiko sat with her eyes closed, letting out a sigh now and then as if she were thinking about something else.

It was bitterly cold for a March night, and we didn't feel much like leaving the warm cocoon of the coffee shop's smoke-filled interior. Our conversation drifted from the uniform issue to boys. Reiko, without naming names, said languidly that nothing was so annoying as a dimwit. I wondered aloud what would have happened if I'd gone on seeing a former boyfriend who was a year ahead of me in school. Whenever this subject came up, Juri would always snort and say, "They're all a bunch of dopes." This time was no different: "Bunch of dopes. Not even worth talking about. I couldn't care less about boys at this point."

We went on in this vein, tossing out comments half to ourselves and cracking up at crass jokes until finally we got up to leave.

It was after ten when I got home. Inside the chilly entrance hall overflowing with packing boxes stood my father, his arms crossed over his chest. I said with all the cheerfulness I could muster, "I'm home!" The muscles in his face tightened in an ugly spasm.

"What the hell time do you think it is? If you like staying out so much, go live by yourself! I'm damned if I'll pay one penny for your upkeep!"

It wasn't the first time he'd yelled at me. The first time it happened I was scared, but after a while I got used to it. Now I stood my ground. I gave the name of one of my classmates – one who passed for a "good girl" – and lied that I'd been over at her house, studying.

Clearly he wasn't buying it. His arms shook. I braced myself, thinking he might slap me, but he did nothing. My mother was standing behind him with a worried look. His temples twitched, but he withdrew into the living room without another word.

That night, after hearing nothing further from him, I spread my bedding out between piles of cardboard boxes alongside my sister, who was in fifth grade.

"Daddy was really mad," she whispered.

"I know," I said.

"He told Mommy to lock the front door and not let you in. She said if you stayed out all night on a cold night like this you'd freeze to death, but he wouldn't listen. Then they started fighting."

"They're married. Married people fight."

"Where were you really?"

"At a jazz place," I said, rolling over. "Smoking and talking about Anpo."[2]

"Oh."

My sister liked to go around mimicking the demonstrators and their slogans: "*Anpo funsai, toso shori!* " Anti-treaty, pro-gress! She did it when my friends came over because it always made them laugh and pay her lots of attention. She thought *anpo funsai* was all one word, but she never asked me what it meant. At what point she figured out its proper meaning, I couldn't say. She's in her thirties now, married with two kids. I never talked about Anpo with her again. She's probably long since forgotten that she ever goofed off in front of her big sister's friends, shouting "*Anpo funsai!* " to cheers and applause.

The impending move meant that she had to give Petey, a pet java sparrow who would come and perch on her finger, to a family down the street. This was clearly weighing heavily on her mind that night, for she went on and on about him.

"You don't think that lady'll give Petey spinach by mistake, do you? Spinach gives him stomachache. He can only eat birdseed and cabbage and mustard spinach and, um, chickweed buds. He can never, *ever* have regular spinach, which I told her, but she's so stupid she'll probably forget. She'll probably go ahead and give it to him and…"

"Go to sleep," I told her. "I'll look in on Petey for you once in a while, and when I do, I'll remind her about the spinach."

She yawned and murmured an assent. I heard sniffling and wondered briefly if she was crying, but then she quieted down. I shut my eyes.

The next afternoon, my parents and sister left Sendai. My aunt and I went to the station in an unseasonable snowstorm to see them

[2] The US-Japan Joint Security Treaty, known in Japanese as *Nichibei anzen hosho juyaku*, or Anpo for short. Opposition to the treaty was a focal point for student protest in the sixties.

off. My father told me to take good care of myself; upset by the previous evening's altercation, he'd gone out of his way all day to be nice. Instead of just nodding, though, I asked him for some spending money. He dug around in his pocket and came up with two thousand-yen bills. "Thank you" would have been embarrassing, so all I said was, "Yay, I'm rich." He smiled bleakly.

After their express train left, my aunt and I stopped by the tea room on the second floor of the Sendai Hotel for some cake. She plied me with questions about school, showing a keen interest. I told her that until recently I'd been head of the Morals Committee – a real whopper – and added that I would probably be getting home late because of after-school activities.

"You're in the school choir, as I recall, aren't you?"

"That's right."

"What do you do after school every day?"

I hadn't had anything to do with the choir for a good six months, but I answered confidently, "Oh, you know. Rehearse for concerts, voice training… all that sort of stuff. I'm head of the soprano section. Sometimes we practice on Sundays, too. The director's pretty gung-ho."

"If you spend that much time on club activities, aren't you afraid of falling behind in your studies?"

"Nope. Never had any trouble before."

"Well, no matter how busy it all keeps you, I want you home on time, all right?"

"Sure," I said, and then asked her what she intended to do if I was ever late. Her small eyes flashed behind the lenses of her glasses and she said without missing a beat, like she'd had the words on the tip of her tongue: "Lock you out of the house."

"Lock me out? Where am I supposed to sleep, then? You mean it's okay if I stay over at a friend's place?"

"Absolutely not. I won't have you acting like a delinquent. You remember the tool shed in the yard? The one Mogu uses for his doghouse? I'll lock you up in there."

I burst out laughing, though inside I was miffed. "Good grief! What am I, two years old? Okay, okay. You don't have to lock me in. I'll sleep there if you want. I'll sleep there every day if it makes you happy."

She leaned forward and said in a strangely serious voice, "Are you sure you ought to say that? There's something you don't know."

"What do you mean?"

She gave an eloquent little laugh. "I can tell you, now that they've gone. Not even your father knows. A girl hanged herself there once."

I laughed dismissively. This tactic was ridiculous – below the belt, and downright childish.

"It's true, Kyoko," she said with a slight frown. Something in the frown struck me as sincere. Despite myself, my flesh crawled.

"It was about ten years ago," she went on. "The daughter of a relative of my late husband spent a year with me. She was just about your age. She'd failed the entrance exam for Tohoku University and spent the year preparing to retake it. Her nerves must have been worn to shreds. One morning, she hanged herself right there in that shed."

It had been a winter morning, she added. Horribly cold. Drool from the dead girl's mouth had formed an icicle.

I shuddered at this last detail, but I wasn't giving in. "In that case, why do you still use the shed? Putting Mogu in it and all. Doesn't it bother you?"

"I did think of tearing it down, but soon after that I got sick and had to go in the hospital. The shed was on my mind, but I simply never got around to doing anything about it. So when I got Mogu, I decided to keep him in there. I thought he might be some comfort to the poor girl's soul."

I mustered a cheerful smile. "Fine by me. Being locked up in a shed where somebody hanged herself won't bother me."

"Oh, no?" She sounded unconvinced. "Even so, it'd be best not to get shut up in a place like that. Just be sure to come home on time."

That was the end of it. Neither of us ever referred to the alleged suicide again. Whether the story was true or not, I still don't know. I probably should have asked around among longtime residents in the neighborhood to see if there was any truth to it, but it never occurred to me.

Now and then I would clean out the shed that doubled as a doghouse. Each time, I would look up at the rafters and wonder which one the girl had used. After dusk, the shadowy rafters seemed like creatures slithering in the dark. Sometimes, imagining what it would be like to see a dead body hanging from them, I was so spooked that I ran out the door. But that didn't happen often. In daylight the rafters all looked alike, and at dusk the faint rays of the evening sun poking through gaps between the weathered boards would light up bits of dog fluff floating in the air with motes of dust, nothing more.

My aunt's house was located at the end of a narrow residential lane lined with dark wooden fences. Her property had the biggest yard and quietest surroundings of all. Just inside the front gate with its latticed sliding door, to the left was a second gate of woven bamboo that opened on a grassy, tree-ringed yard with a flower garden. Here Mogu, her Shiba dog, roamed in the daytime on the alert for moles and frogs like the faithful guard he was.

In my uncle's day the house had been an elegant residence in the traditional style. After he died, my aunt embarked on a new life as a piano teacher, and had the house extensively remodeled with many Western touches. Painted light pink on the outside, the smallish one-storey structure now suffered from a lack of individuality, I thought, but it did have warmth and an air of pleasant domesticity about it.

There were six rooms in all: a soundproofed piano room with adjacent sunroom, a living room, my aunt's bedroom, a little room that contained nothing but a paulownia chest, and a parlour. That was it. I was assigned the parlour, beside the entryway. Despite its name, it was really just a sort of storage room piled with things like electric fans no longer in use and gift sets of soft drinks. My aunt said she'd be happy to see me put it to proper use.

The room wasn't bad at all. It was medium-sized, with windows on the east and south that let in plenty of sunlight. The south window looked out on a little covered terrace where I could picture myself sitting in a rattan chair of a summer afternoon, engrossed in a book. Best of all, I had the room all to myself, a place of my own where my aunt couldn't interfere, for which I was grateful.

The bay window to the east offered a view of the garden tool shed. As I looked out at the old shed, a solitary annex beyond the lawn and the flower garden, it seemed jarringly out of place. I stacked books and notebooks in front of that window so that no one could open it. Just outside was a hydrangea bush, and sometimes after dark, lit by the light at the gate, its leaves would cast peculiar, dim shadows on the glass, as if something pale and sinister floating in the air had stuck fast to the pane.

I got my aunt to hang a heavy curtain at the window. Why I wanted it, I didn't say.

This was how I began my final year of high school. Every morning I got up on time and set off for school, and every night I was back promptly at seven. I rarely attended all six classes in the day. Once every three days I arranged with Juri and Reiko to leave school early. Not that we gave our homeroom teacher proper notice and went straight home, as the rules required. We were the school troublemakers, probably blacklisted by the Municipal Education Committee; a note from any of us requesting early release would have been given short shrift.

The proper term for what we did was not "leaving school early" but "breaking out." The school was blocked off on three sides by high hills, like a prison, with only one main entrance. To make things harder, in order to go outside you had to pass the window of the teachers' room. There was always a teacher or two posted there as a lookout, and scrunching down to try to make yourself invisible wasn't any use.

The only way to escape was to climb the high hill behind the school, go along the fence, and come out on the road where a bus went by. The three of us used to scramble through the dense underbrush, making our way up like rock climbers, not caring when our skirts lifted in the wind. Reiko was the least athletic of us, and every time she climbed the hill she'd give little cries that sounded exactly like the piping shrieks of child kabuki actors. Juri and I would have to pull her along by the hand to keep her quiet.

It used to take us more than twenty minutes to reach the road, I remember. Before boarding the bus we would clean ourselves up, brushing dry grass and clumps of dirt from the back of each other's skirts. There were always plenty of seats. We would sit on the long bench at the back of the bus and celebrate our successful getaway with whoops of triumph.

Our classmates never ratted on us to the teachers. Maybe they got a vicarious thrill from our escapades. Some would even lend us a hand, but others would lay bets about how long it would be before we were suspended from school. Back then the three of us were hell-bent on doing things that nobody else could or would do. Others may have rolled their eyes at our juvenile feats of derring-do, but they were certainly never bored by us, of that I'm sure.

We were like actors playing roles we thought ourselves uniquely equipped for. Roles that meant rejecting, at all costs, any conception of ourselves as girls of good family, or model students, or "nice." Of course it wasn't until much later that I realized it was all an act. Certainly at the time we were dead serious. Still, I'm proud of having lived like that, even for a brief time.

After escaping from school we would usually go to the park, or the student cafeteria of Tohoku University, or a jazz coffee shop. There was always something going on in the park back then, the food in the student cafeteria was amazingly cheap, and in the coffee shops we'd often run into high school or college kids we knew. From them we learned in vivid detail how to hold rallies in school and print up leaflets, as well as things to keep in mind when taking over the podium to make a radical speech. Guys from various radical factions invited us to their meetings, and we took them up on it. We went to many campus demonstrations, too.

After all this time, I can't remember what it was we discussed so intently. What did we have to say? What point were we trying to get across? There was the Vietnam War, and there was Anpo. There was the Okinawa reversion issue, too. Activists were always coming up from Tokyo to try and get us organized. There were folk song rallies and rabble-rousing speeches and street demonstrations. I walked willingly into the turmoil those people stirred up, saying the same things they said, doing the same things they did, writing the same things they wrote. I was no better than a monkey, aping whatever they did. I didn't really care two cents about their Vietnam or their Anpo or their Okinawa. I didn't care about Marx or Stalin or revolution, either. I didn't want to devote myself to politics and revolution. I didn't like the people who showed off their threadbare knowledge in endless, empty debates. I hated the girls who fell in love with radical students, confused romance with political comradeship, and purposely wore dirty clothes to take handmade lunches to young men entrenched behind barricades.

Yet I treasured the hours I spent with these people, with their endless, empty debates. I felt a helpless sympathy for the girls who had sex with their activist lovers inside barricades or gave shelter to their injured boyfriends, tenderly ministering to wounds suffered in demonstrations.

I was glad to be rushing headlong into the storm. I couldn't sit still. I couldn't spend my time listening to music, reading books for pleasure, and studying to get into a Tokyo university. I'd go crazy, I thought. Not knowing where else to go, I longed to escape from my present circumstances, from myself. Maybe that was the whole reason why, day after day, I broke out of school and took part in demonstrations I scarcely understood, showed off my own threadbare knowledge.

Monkey see, monkey do. Oh, that was me, all right. Often I felt ashamed. Even now it makes me blush to remember. But I never let on about it. Probably lots of them felt the same way I did, and suffered equally from self-loathing. Juri and Reiko and all my other close friends, every last one. Thinking this helps a little. At least it allows me to be kind.

2

During the week of holidays at the beginning of May, my mother came to Sendai to see how I was doing, and stayed two nights at my aunt's house. It was just when a huge anti-war folk song rally was being staged at the big park downtown. I racked my brains for a way to slip away.

Why anybody sang such dreadful songs they couldn't imagine, agreed my mother and aunt, hoping to discourage me, but I responded by lying that one of the guitar players was the image of John Lennon. "He's really cool. A lot of the kids in my class go to folk song rallies just to see him. Somebody even got his autograph."

"That John what's-his-name, he's in variety, isn't he?" My aunt, who only knew classical music, lumped the Beatles in with traditional *enka* singers like Haruo Minami. I stifled a laugh, and said only, "No, he's a musician."

"I see. And you say the guitar player looks like him?"

"Yes. A college student."

"A student giving out autographs? Ridiculous," snorted my mother.

"I've never actually seen him. Reiko and I are going today just to take a look."

"Mind that's all you do," said my aunt, with severe distaste. "You girls should not be listening to those awful songs."

Mother looked as if she wanted to say more, but I skipped out to meet Reiko as promised, then headed for the park with her. When I mentioned what my aunt had said about John Lennon being in variety, she stopped in the middle of the street to laugh, clutching her sides. Reiko didn't laugh often, but when she did it pealed out like a bell. It was contagious, and I joined in.

It was a magnificently clear day, the afternoon sky a piercing blue. Tall cedars encircling the park looked like big green ice-cream cones. The breeze was dry and warm, and faintly scented with flowers.

"So anyway," said Reiko, wiping tears of laughter from her eyes, "tell me something – do you like classical music?"

"Yeah, it's okay. Why?"

"There's a place I want to take you afterwards."

"A classical music place?"

"A café that goes in for baroque music, as a matter of fact. It's really different, you'll see. It looks like a hangout for student activists, but it's not. Although some do go there. The time I went, a bunch of people from the League of Communists were there, muttering away, but there were lots of other people too, sitting around like zombies."

"What kind of people?"

"Oh, I don't know. Aspiring poets and writers, maybe, or maybe just apolitical types with no money and nothing better to do. Anyway, they all sit there smoking and reading. It's hilarious, you've got to see it. The seats all face the front like on a train. There's nothing else. Just zombies sitting on train seats not saying a word. And all the time, baroque music is pouring out of these huge speakers at top volume. Let's go, just for fun."

"What's it called?" I asked.

"A Cappella," said Reiko, tossing her gorgeous mane of hair. She giggled. "Great name, don't you think?"

I agreed that it was, and asked her who she'd gone there with. Her only answer was a vague smile.

When we reached the park, the rally was in full swing, with a large number of young people sitting around on the grass singing protest songs. Youths in helmets were delivering speeches in the open auditorium. The air was filled with the cacophony of their voices, mixed with strains of 'We Shall Overcome.' Reiko and I walked around the park, stepping on littered handbills, hunting for Juri.

The flowerbeds were a riot of pansies. Beyond them we spotted Juri in black cotton slacks, waving and coming towards us. Under one arm was a ten-gallon hat she'd been using to collect donations.

"Any luck?" I asked, going up to her.

She nodded. "Today's great. Everybody's feeling generous. I've got nearly three hundred yen so far."

"That'll pay for three cups of coffee," said Reiko.

"Don't be stupid. This is for the struggle."

"Relax. It'll pay for three coffees at A Cappella."

"What's that?" asked Juri, squinting in the bright sunshine. Reiko gave the same description she'd given me. Juri grunted noncommittally, then said, "Sure, what the heck. Shall I scrounge up some more funds, then? I'm starving. Might as well get enough for a bowl of ramen apiece while we're at it."

"Send Reiko," I said with a wink. "She'll do the job all right. One wiggle of her hips should be enough."

Juri agreed with a coarse laugh, but Reiko backed off in alarm. "No! You can't make me!"

"There's nothing to it, don't worry. Anyway, you're a member of the struggle committee, right? This is an order from your committee leader. Go forth."

"What do I tell people? I don't know what to say."

"Just make it up. Tell them you represent the Committee for the Struggle to Abolish School Uniforms, a division of the Antiwar Association at your high school. You're raising funds for the cause and you'd be grateful for any contribution they could make. You can say that, can't you?"

"What if someone asks how we plan to use the money?"

Juri grimaced. "God, you're a numbskull. Tell them it's to print up handbills. Wait, undo one more button on your blouse. Now go on out and strut your stuff."

Reiko puffed out her cheeks with distaste, but Juri and I paid no attention, shoving the ten-gallon hat into her hands. Muttering to herself, she ventured onto the grass. "Good luck," I called after her. The line of her back, as lithe as a cat's, melted into the crowd on the other side of the flowerbeds.

Reiko had once attempted suicide. She told me about it herself. It had happened the previous summer, before we were especially close. There are always one or two oddballs in any class, and that was how she'd seemed to me – just another odd fish. She was pretty, with amazingly good skin and mature features, but she lacked the trust-building traits that mean so much to most teenagers – things like joining in, straightforwardness, effort and perseverance.

She never went out of her way to be friends with anyone, generally spending her free time alone with her nose in a book, yet she didn't seem isolated either. She wasn't annoying, so people just naturally accepted her. She was like a cat curled on the hearth, always nearby, seldom making any noise, asserting her presence in a quiet way.

When I talked nonsense with Juri, Reiko had a way of sitting by us and looking on with slitted eyes. Juri had a bit of a mean streak, and sometimes she'd say, "Know what, Reiko? You look like some kinda reptile." Reiko never took offense, just murmured, "Do I now?" with a wry smile.

In some ways the description wasn't far off the mark. Reiko did have a kind of animal instinct, and perhaps that's why she chose me to open up to. One fall day after school, at the beginning of the second term of our second year, in a corner of a deserted earth science classroom, she unburdened herself to me.

"Have you ever heard of Hyminal?" she asked.

"It's a sleeping pill, right?"

"Right. Did you ever try chewing it?"

"Nope. I've never taken it."

"No, I suppose not. You… wouldn't need to."

I was silent. There was something ominous in her tone. Outside the window some girls were practicing soft tennis on the tennis court. As I waited for her to go on, I watched the ball fly back and forth through the air.

After a beat, she said, "The longer you chew it, the sweeter it tastes. It's bizarre. You take a mouthful, chew and chew, and it turns sweet in your mouth. Not bitter in the least."

"So you were having insomnia?"

She laughed weakly. "What a nice person you are. Actually, they're good for a lot of different symptoms. Just so you know, I'll tell you. They're just the thing when you want to go to sleep and never wake up, when you want to forget everything. Do give it a try if you're so inclined, you'll see."

Reiko had a habit of saying things like that: "Do give it a try if you're so inclined," or "Fare thee well," or "Would that it were." Expressions that might have come from the bored heroine of some novel of bourgeois decadence – yet funnily enough, when she said them, they didn't sound out of place.

With a little laugh, she added, "But then, you probably don't ever feel like going to sleep and never waking up, do you, Kyoko? You're so full of life."

"You mean you tried to kill yourself by taking Hyminal?"

"Don't look so shocked. Girls who try to off themselves are a dime a dozen and you know it."

"When? When did you do it?"

"During summer vacation, one night when it was so hot I was going out of my mind. When I came to, my father was there beside me, and behind him was my mother, whimpering. The inside of my mouth tasted awful and my breath smelled foul. A nurse came up to me and said, like she was angry with me, 'Young lady, I just cleaned out your stomach. Don't you ever mess it up like that again.' It made me laugh out loud. I mean, it was just so funny. As if she'd been running a vacuum cleaner around my insides or something." She smiled mirthlessly.

"What made you do it?" I asked softly.

"Lord knows," she answered, as if it didn't concern her. "Boredom, probably. I was bored to death."

There had to have been something else, I thought, but I didn't press her. For a while we looked out together in silence at the white ball sailing to and fro over the net. A chilly autumn wind blew in through the open window.

I said, "So are you… better now?"

She nodded.

"How's your appetite?"

"Fine. Really, I'm completely back to normal."

"Good."

She looked at me through slitted eyes in that way of hers, and gave a tiny laugh.

From then on, Reiko, Juri and I were best friends. I didn't ask anything more about her attempted suicide, and she never brought it up again. Sometimes she would sit and brood. No matter what I said to her then, she would only look away despondently, but she always snapped out of it in a few days and became her old self again.

Her three preoccupations were *chansons*, French movies, and suicide. Sometimes she wrote gorgeous decadent poetry. She seemed

. far more grown up than me, as if her experience of love was miles beyond mine, but she never spoke about it – though sometimes when we talked, she gave off an aura of such heavy sensuality that her words seemed to linger in the air a moment like cartoon balloons before disappearing. Maybe this was a knack she'd deliberately developed to make herself stand out. In reality she was a sweet young thing, more vulnerable than anyone else, and in need of an anchor.

A tall man with long hair hanging down his back was having an earnest debate with two shorter men. Reiko went over to them, casting a halfhearted glance back at Juri and me. We smiled encouragingly and gave her the thumbs-up. She said something timid to the three men, and their faces brightened as they looked at her. I could see her face turn rosy pink. She was beautiful.

As she spoke, they each nodded and reached into a pocket. The coins they tossed into the ten-gallon hat gleamed for a second in the sun. She smiled with some strain. The tall scraggly one scratched his head, opened his mouth and laughed.

Reiko came back giggling, her lips pursed, her cheeks still flushed. "Look! Five hundred yen in one fell swoop. The two shorter guys gave a hundred yen apiece, but the tall one chipped in three hundred!"

Juri whooped. "I knew you could do it! You're the greatest, Reiko. Let's go out for some miso ramen later."

"Look over there, Kyoko," said Reiko in excitement, grabbing me by the arm. "Don't you think the tall guy is cute?"

I craned my neck to look at him. He struck me as pretty ordinary, a bit of a hick in fact. The long hair did gave him a certain air, but if he ever cut it short I had a feeling he'd look like a plucked chicken, and I said so. "Hmm, I wonder," said Reiko. For a while she kept glancing back at him, but eventually slumped down as if she'd lost interest.

For perhaps an hour after that we joked with people at the rally, sang songs, smoked, and ran into a lit major who offered the use of his department's Struggle Committee headquarters to run off handbills all night long, any time we wanted.

"Help yourself to the copying machine," he said. "You'll have to supply your own paper, though."

"No problem," I said.

"How many do you need to run off?"

"Enough for the whole student body, over three hundred at least."

"Three hundred at one time? You're talking about hours of work! You might as well sleep there, then. It's no great shakes, but there's a sofa you can use."

We thanked him and left the park.

The air felt close and muggy. After only a short walk we were covered in sweat. We crossed the big avenue in front of the park and walked around the shopping area, which was busier than usual, filled with families out taking advantage of the week of holidays at the beginning of May.

As we passed in front of a little record store, we heard strains of 'Hey Jude' coming from inside. Reiko stood still and hummed along. She checked out the shop window while Juri urged her to hurry up. Reiko nodded expressionlessly and meandered on with all the energy of a hooker closing up shop.

As I walked along, my thoughts turned idly to the entrance exam looming nine months ahead. I'd done little or no studying – worse still, I was in danger of flunking out. I came home on time every evening and went straight to my room. I stayed up late, so as far as my aunt knew I was hitting the books, but I spent my time silently turning things over in my mind. It's hard to explain just what my thoughts were, but for the most part it was plain woolgathering. I'd start thinking about A, which led to B, and before reaching any conclusion I'd move on to C… that sort of thing.

I slept in snatches. Since I never got eight solid hours of sleep, my brain was always fuzzy. To clear the haze I wrote poem after poem and even kept a sort of journal, but it did no good. I should have just gone to bed and slept all I wanted. But I liked sitting up late at night in my room, listening to records while I imagined setting foot in an unknowable future. Sleep was impossible, since there was never enough time to think about the real-life problems in front of me – entrance exams, graduation, leaving for college – all packaged conveniently together like a box of assorted goodies.

Past Fujisaki Department Store, just between there and the arcade, we came across a young man selling books of self-published poetry that he'd spread out around him on the ground. His face was abnormally pale and smooth, but the collar of his shirt was grimy and he had a slightly soiled look overall. We walked past him with our eyes on the books of poetry, and he suddenly darted a solemn look at me. I gave him a little smile, but he merely twitched his mouth in token response.

The poems had been mimeographed on cheap paper and stapled together. The cover bore the words *Beacon Fire* in stiff lettering. Scrawled on the concrete in chalk were the words "100 yen each." I was halted by a surge of unreasonable affection for this fellow who was spending the sunny holiday afternoon not at the folk song rally or on a date, but hawking these useless poetry collections.

I reached into my shoulder bag and brought out my wallet. "One, please," I said. He nodded and said in a barely audible voice, "Thanks." I took out 150 yen and handed it to him. "An extra donation."

He acknowledged this only with a brief nod. I picked up one of the poetry collections and stuck it in my shoulder bag. A passing breeze carried the faint cries of someone at the university delivering an impassioned protest speech.

"Poetry nut, huh," teased Juri.

"That's me," I said.

If not for that impulsive purchase, I might never have spoken to Wataru Domoto in A Cappella. A strange thought. Even allowing that encounters with other people are the result of infinite small overlapping coincidences, the direct cause often seems to be an even more tenuous coincidence, an event so perfectly commonplace that it barely registers at the time.

Poetry of all kinds appealed to me. My eyes were drawn irresistibly to the writing of contemporary wordsmiths who assuaged their loneliness with a stream of verbal diarrhea. When I saw someone selling a collection of poetry on the street, I nearly always bought it; when asked to purchase a self-published magazine filled with what I would now call narcissistic treacle, I did. Had I not acquired this habit early on, I probably wouldn't have bought that poetry collection that day, and so it wouldn't have transpired that while sitting in a coffee shop on a seat suffused with the smell of cigarettes I opened the booklet titled *Beacon Fire*. Without that, there'd have been no reason for me to have a conversation with Wataru Domoto.

The basement place specializing in baroque music where Reiko took Juri and me was disconcertingly drab. Inside a mere cubbyhole were rows of seats covered in cheap imitation leather, all facing forward. In the back there was just one booth where four people could sit face to face. The front wall had ceiling high built-in speakers. Not one picture adorned the sooty light brown walls. All there was to see were a handful of customers hunched over like train passengers.

Solemn baroque music was playing at high volume, with the low vibrations of a pipe organ sounding peculiarly quiet. Even a sigh seemed likely to set off vibrations around the room.

"What the hell is this?" said Juri aloud. Reiko shushed her reprovingly. On the wall to the right of the entrance hung a cardboard sign marked "Please talk quietly." Juri and I exchanged commiserating looks as we followed Reiko into A Cappella.

There were just four empty places in the middle section and two on the right. The booth was taken. The seats were all in pairs, so the three of us couldn't sit together in any case. I let Juri and Reiko sit together, and took a seat behind them.

I couldn't really tell if the place felt congenial or not. The coffee, when it came, was bitter and flavorless. My ears, accustomed to jazz, found the music overly formal, reminiscent of the snobbish Classical Collection records that my aunt sometimes played in the living room.

In the seat in front of me, Juri and Reiko were passing notes back and forth. Now and then Juri would let loose with a belly laugh, and Reiko would put her head down on the table to stifle her laughter. Behind me, a couple of high school boys were talking in low murmurs.

Reiko passed back the notebook she and Juri were using for their messages. It had the question "So what's your verdict?" written in it with a fine-point mechanical pencil. I scribbled "Not bad" and handed it back. She turned around and whispered, "Check the walls. See the row of dark, round smudges? Apparently that's from customers leaning their heads there."

She was right. On the wall by every row of seats was a stain the approximate shape of a human head.

"Gross," said Juri. "You mean those are from people's hair oil and dandruff?"

"Ssh," said Reiko, pursing her lips. We exchanged suppressed giggles and all faced forward again.

I took out the handmade poetry book I'd just bought and opened it to the first page, where lines of tiny, stiff lettering crowded together in uniform size. Words like "fictitious," "gravestone," "skeptical," and "inaction" were written in a cramped, nervous hand that slanted up to the right. The poet's name appeared in block letters: "T. TAMAZAWA."

I couldn't tell if the poems were good or bad. Never could. I was and always had been a terrible judge of poetry, as I was completely lacking in any standards by which to decide if something – not just poetry – was superior or mediocre. Immature words, pedantic words, words that attested to their owner's conceit and inferiority complex... I enjoyed the sight of them all. Looking at clumps of hopelessly bad, stupid writing was somehow comforting. The more foolish a poem was, the more I liked the poet. Anyone who was crazy enough to stand on a street corner selling his grubby, hard-won mental excreta won a special place in my heart.

At some point, I wasn't sure how long, the door opened and some people came in. I could feel the pleasantly stagnant air in the room start flowing outdoors, and I looked in that direction.

A girl entered, followed by two guys. Her hair was cut boyishly short like Cecile, the lead character in the movie *Bonjour Tristesse*. Shaking her head, she swept the room with a challenging gaze. Big eyes, small mouth, a face with off-kilter charm. Though on the small side, she was instantly noticeable. She strode over to the empty seats across from Juri and Reiko and beckoned. The taller boy sat down next to her, and the other one unhesitatingly slid in next to me. As he did I caught a whiff of something dry, like hay. I looked back down at the poetry.

The room was quiet. Stately court music was playing, and no one made a sound. The boy beside me sat motionless for a while with his arms folded, but when his coffee came, he softly cleared his throat.

"That isn't Tamazawa's stuff you have there by any chance, is it?" I looked up, and he gave me a nice smile. "It is, isn't it?"

Like a backward grammar school pupil, I turned to the table of contents, found the name "T. TAMAZAWA," and awkwardly held it out to show him.

"I knew it," he said, grinning. "He's a classmate of mine at college."

I said, "Oh," then added more politely, "Is that so?" He definitely looked older than me. He was no high school kid, that was immediately apparent.

For the briefest instance our eyes met in the dull yellow light. Somehow dazzled, I slid my eyes away.

It's hard for me to describe him. The first word that came to mind at the time was "Jewish." Not that I'd ever actually known anyone who was Jewish; I'd never even seen any Jews, except in photographs. Still, that's what I thought. It might have been the combination of his glossy forehead and the lock of dark, wavy hair that hung down on it. Or his chiseled features, so untypical of a Japanese, and perfectly straight mouth. To me he fitted to a T the image of Jewish attractiveness that I'd picked up from photos and movies.

"Where'd you run into Tamazawa?" he asked, taking a cigarette from a wrinkled package of Short Hope and lighting it with a match.

Flustered, I pointed like a child at the wall. "Over there, near Fujisaki Department Store."

He laughed, waved out the match and tossed it into the ashtray. "So he's still at it, selling jerk-off. What a hopeless case. And you paid good money? A hundred yen?"

I nodded. "A hundred and fifty, actually. I threw in the extra fifty as a donation."

"Takes all kinds. Fifty yen for a spoiled street-corner poet?"

"It's all right. My friends and I have taken plenty of people for a ride, soliciting donations and then spending it all on snacks."

Overhearing this, Reiko turned around and grinned. I indicated her and Juri with a jerk of my chin. "That's them. The three of us are always up to no good."

"High school?" he asked.

I nodded and held up three fingers. "Third year, S. Girls' High School."

"This is Kyoko Noma," Reiko told him. "Our school's very own Red Rosa."[1]

"Well, well, well," he said, his eyes widening with interest. "How

---

[1] Rosa Luxemburg (1871–1919) was a German revolutionary leader.

about that!" But I could tell that this was an automatic response. He sounded like an adult praising a child for some minor achievement. Annoyed, I turned my head to one side.

"Another Red Rosa. That *is* something," he said in a conciliatory tone.

"No, it isn't," I said flatly. "It's just a figure of speech."

"So S. Girls' High School has joined the anti-war coalition?"

"Nothing that structured," I said. "We're protesting against school uniforms, appealing for the right to wear our own clothes to school."

"And you're the ringleader?"

"I am."

"You give protest speeches?"

"I haven't yet, but I expect to before long."

"So you're a protest leader who buys poetry from street-corner poets, makes rabble-rousing speeches, and attends rallies and demonstrations. Must be exciting."

"What?"

"Why, everything."

I laughed sardonically. "Stop talking down to me, will you, please?"

"I didn't mean to," he said with a smile, then dropped his eyes forlornly. "Sorry. No offense meant."

The quick apology caught me off guard. I closed the poetry collection, put it back in my purse, and stuck a cigarette in my mouth. He handed me a box of matches, but I thanked him politely and lit it with a match of my own.

Bastard, I thought, with no idea why. He was just some guy I'd never seen before. He hadn't said anything to get miffed about, really. He'd been perfectly nice. But clearly he was immune to the epidemic that was then raging like measles among young people – a wave of war protests, demonstrations, rallies and skirmishes. Why that should have bothered me, I didn't know.

I puffed away in silence. He took out a black fountain pen from his shirt pocket and removed the cap. Then he slid the paper coaster from under his glass of water and wrote something on it: "Canon." The blue-black ink quickly blurred, making the letters stand out big and bold.

He held up the coaster so that his friends across the aisle could see it. As the long-faced fellow looked at it and nodded expressionlessly,

I had my first good look at him. His face was chillingly cold and handsome. An unhappy face, I thought. Smooth skin, brown hair slicked straight back, thin knife-slash lips. Nothing remotely like what might be called an expression.

The girl with the Cecile haircut said teasingly, "Come on, Wataru! The Canon, again? Don't you ever get tired of it?" No, said the boy called Wataru, he didn't. She shrugged impishly, gave me a sideways glance, and looked ahead again.

Wataru handed the coaster to a mustachioed, bearlike waiter who silently disappeared with it.

"You'll hear some good music now," he said to me unexpectedly. "I just requested Pachelbel's Canon."

"Pachelbel?"

"Never heard of him?"

I admitted that I hadn't. Again his eyes widened slightly in wonder. "Is that so strange?" I asked.

Smiling faintly, he slowly shook his head. His amazingly dark eyes were fixed on me. Playing the part of a wanton delinquent, I cocked my head back and blew out a stream of smoke at the ceiling. He said no more.

Soon the music that had been playing came to an end and a faint rasp sounded over the speakers as the needle came down on the next record. Pachelbel's Canon turned out to be a quiet, lovely piece of music. The high tones of the violins chased endlessly after softly reverberating low tones, with the in-and-out motion of waves. I was entranced, pleasantly paralyzed, as if the core of my body had grown heavy. I took a deep breath. It was as though I'd heard this music somewhere before, and yet was hearing it for the first time.

Thinking that some comment was required, I turned my head to look at him. "It's pretty," I said, and instantly regretted it. Why couldn't I have come up with something more profound? The corners of his mouth jerked in acknowledgment and he inclined his head perceptibly, but he didn't meet my eyes.

When the music finished playing, Juri looked back and said, "Want to go now? I'm pretty hungry."

I nodded and got up. The boy wasn't looking at us. He'd started whispering to his friend across the aisle. The girl with the Cecile haircut was smoking a cigarette with an air of boredom. The long-faced guy then looked up at us, and Wataru did too.

"See ya," I said. I meant it to sound harsh, but to my chagrin it came out sounding merely childish.

Wataru murmured, "Goodbye."

When we went outside, Reiko asked, "Who was that?"

"How do I know?" I said, surprised at the sharpness of my tone. "Just some smart-alecky college student."

"Kind of cute, wasn't he?" she said. "Although the other one, the one sitting with the girl, is more my type. But I'll bet you liked the guy next to you more, didn't you? I can always tell."

"Not especially," I said, and added loudly, "Ramen, here we come."

The three of us set off for our usual place and ate our usual miso ramen. By the time I'd finished my bowlful, I'd forgotten all about the boy named Wataru.

3

They're not made anymore, but I used to be partial to a brand of cigarettes called "MF." They tasted of mint. Back then people believed that mint-flavored cigarettes could cause impotence, so most MF smokers were female. By the age of seventeen I was up to half a pack a day. Smoking gave me palpitations and pressure in my chest, and made my head swim. The sensation felt vaguely like dying. The idea that my smoker friends and I all soothed our overwrought nerves with the taste of death seems pretty stupid now. As I recall, we were constantly pulling out cigarettes, one after another, like starving children sucking on sweets. Cigarettes weren't merely an accessory, but a wonder drug that absorbed our excess energy.

One rainy Sunday in late June I bought a pack of MF, slipped it in the skirt pocket of my jumper and walked around town. I'd stepped out early in the afternoon, telling my aunt that I was going to buy an exam study guide. I had nothing to do, but couldn't sit still. Holding an umbrella, I wandered around town, picked up a paperback by Yukio Mishima at a bookstore, and went on walking, book in hand.

May and June had swept by like a sandstorm. As promised, the student we'd met at the folk song rally let us borrow a copying machine to print up hundreds of handbills. Early the next morning we sneaked into school and laid them on the students' desks. Nearly half were confiscated by staff members who realized something was going on, but the rest got through. The faculty raised a hue and cry, but the more they carried on, the more they fanned the students' excitement.

We took over the gymnasium and held an emergency all-school assembly. Juri gave a speech while Reiko and I, with the rest of the struggle committee, barricaded the doors with tables and chairs to keep the teachers out. The students went wild with excitement, but we three stayed calm. Juri's speech was terrific. In my mind's eye I can still see her up on the platform in front of the arrayed students, gripping the hand mike as she talked. She was calm, practical, and thoroughly convincing. She showed no sign of weakness, she had plenty of confidence, and above all, she was impeccably rational.

Several days after the assembly, the principal sent a letter to my father in Tokyo. Dad immediately telephoned my aunt. I got summoned to the phone for a tongue-lashing. "You're no daughter of mine," he yelled. "Is that so?" I said. My aunt, who was at my side listening, snatched the receiver away and assured my father indignantly that it was all a mistake of some kind. "Our Kyoko would never do such a thing!"

I could hear my mother's voice on the other end of the line, too. The three adults talked for a long time, taking turns grabbing the two receivers in Sendai and Tokyo. I got up, went back to my room and put on a record. My aunt came and knocked on the door, but I didn't open it. I didn't want to talk to anyone.

The assembly that had turned into such a cauldron of excitement ended lamely, with only a three-day suspension for Juri and me. For those three days we made a point of going to school in our regular clothes. While everyone else was in class, we sat on a bench in the schoolyard and looked at the sky. The teachers frowned with disapproval but said nothing. At lunchtime, Reiko brought us some pork-cutlet sandwiches and orange juice. We ate them and then spent all afternoon, too, looking up at the sky.

The injury I suffered in a street demonstration on June 15th was in part, I think, an offshoot of these developments. For two full months, I'd done nothing that could remotely be called studying for exams. My attitude of utter negligence may have left me somehow vulnerable.

The day it happened, the demonstration had just ended and we were singing an international protest song. All of a sudden there was a shrill metallic screech, and the riot police attacked. A male student nearby yelled, "Run for it!" and gave me a shove from behind. I tried blindly to flee. Blood spurted, someone groaned. I turned around to see the same student sitting hunched over on the ground, bleeding from the mouth and getting hit on the head.

The next moment I was pushed off balance, then someone grabbed my leg, sending me crashing to the ground. The next thing

I knew I was at the bottom of a pile of human dominoes. I shrank into myself, trembling half in fear of being arrested and half in concern that I might die on the spot. I became a weak and helpless girl. In front of my eyes I could see the shoes of panicky students running for dear life. I could see the duralumin shields of the riot police. Beyond the shoes and the shields and the blood, I could see the street and a shred of blue sky. My eyes clouded over with tears and I cried like a baby.

The pain in my back and my arm didn't go away. I was sure I'd broken something, but scarier than the pain was the possibility that my aunt might find out. It wasn't her I feared so much as her telling my father. I stayed in my room that night, pretending to study, and thrashed around in pain on my bed. The next day Juri went with me to the school nurse, who stared aghast at my wounds. Juri and I played it down, telling her I'd tripped and fallen.

She gave me a compress for my sprained elbow and something for the pain. While she wasn't looking, Juri swiped another dozen pills and slipped them into the pocket of my uniform.

I ripped my bloodstained blouse to shreds and burned it in the backyard with the trash so my aunt wouldn't find it. I felt worn out. From then on I stopped going to demonstrations. The very word made me bolt. In the end I was just a smart-mouthed know-it-all, a coward with brains. I'd always vaguely suspected as much, but it was galling to face the truth. Still, there it was. This was what happened to girls like me who didn't give a damn about Vietnam or the Security Treaty. I'd had it coming.

Around this time I began to think of letting Juri take over as chairman of the Struggle Committee, of giving up all my activism. It was with a sense of faint dread that I'd spent that rainy Sunday wandering around town. Despite my umbrella, the gentle rain soaked into my short-sleeve blouse. Before I knew it, I found myself standing in front of A Cappella.

I'd been there twice already since Reiko took us. Both times I'd gone alone. I could read a book there or, better yet, just sit and think without interruption or jot my thoughts down in a notebook. A couple of times I ran into acquaintances there, but we didn't talk much. I would sit with my head against a wall stain formed by the oily heads of countless others before me. As I sat motionless with my head pressed against the dark blotch, I felt strangely at ease.

That June afternoon I folded my umbrella and went down the narrow stairs, rounding my back. Even the stairway reeked of smoke, and I could hear the quiet, pervasive tones of a harpsichord. I pushed the door open.

The interior was thick with cigarette smoke. Several men glanced my way. I looked around and saw no one I recognized. The seats were almost all occupied, with only the booth at the rear completely empty. Rather than share a seat with someone, I sat down in the booth. Two boys were sitting in front of it with their backs to me. One of them turned around slowly and gave me a smile.

I felt my face turn a bright crimson. I could only wonder why I blushed so easily.

The Jewish-looking boy – Wataru – was looking at me. I swiveled the umbrella handle and tried to return his smile, but succeeded only in twisting my mouth in a funny way. Without turning my head I moved my eyes to his face. His friend with the slicked-back hair turned and said a quiet "Hi."

"You came alone today?" asked Wataru.

"Yes," I said, nodding. "We meet quite a lot here, don't we?"

"It's only the second time, isn't it?" he said.

"I'm not so sure about that," I said archly. I wanted to sound arch the way grownup women did, but it didn't come off.

"It's definitely the second time," said his friend. "We haven't seen you since the May holidays."

"Oh, yeah," I said quickly, nodding. "That's right."

"You here to meet someone?"

"No."

"Is there something you were planning to do here?"

I didn't understand the question, so I sat with a silly smile on my face and blinked. Wataru said encouragingly, as if humoring a younger sister, "You know, read a book, sit and think, listen to some music?"

"Not especially."

"Then we aren't bothering you."

"No."

"Mind if we join you?" he asked, pointing. "We're bored anyway. It'd be great to chat with the Red Rosa of S. Girls' High."

I said nothing, so they picked up their coffee cups, got up, and took the seats across from me. Wataru was wearing an emerald green summer sweater, and his companion had on a white polo shirt, the top button open to reveal light-colored chest hair. They sat side by side and looked me over as curiously as if I'd been a rabbit in a pet shop.

"Was the protest speech a success?" asked Wataru. He wasn't exactly teasing, but he didn't sound completely serious, either.

"It went okay," I said, and ordered some coffee from the mustachioed waiter, who set a glass of water in front of me and left. I took a sip of water and pulled my cigarettes from my skirt pocket.

"You said you were a third-year student, right?" said Wataru, reaching out to light my cigarette with a match. "So that makes you what, eighteen?"

"Seventeen," I said, adding politely that I could light my own cigarette, thanks anyway. "My birthday's in November, so I'm not eighteen yet."

"Same age as Ema," said the boy with the slicked-back hair, half to himself.

"Who's Ema?"

"The girl who was here with us the other day," he said. "Remember her? Big doll-like eyes."

"Right." I nodded, remembering. The face of the girl with the Cecile haircut, smoking a cigarette in a sexy way, flitted across my mind. "Your girlfriend."

He nodded and gave a knowing chuckle.

"You two make a nice couple."

"Why, thank you." He looked at Wataru, and Wataru looked at me.

"We learned your name before," said Wataru. "That pretty girl with the long hair told us what it was."

"Her name's Reiko. The other one is Juri."

"And you're… Kyoko, right?"

"Lucky guess," I said, but the knowledge that he had remembered my name after hearing it once two months ago made me squirm with embarrassment. Hurriedly, gabbling my way through the story, I told them about having to stand next to my name on the blackboard and bow every time I changed schools. They laughed in appreciation.

They were both much more relaxed this time. The one with his hair slicked back and his chest hair showing, especially, looked a lot more at ease than the time before. It occurred to me briefly that perhaps he and Ema had quarreled that day.

They introduced themselves. Wataru's full name was Wataru Domoto, and his friend told me he was called Yunosuke Seki. They were juniors at Tohoku University, had been classmates since high school, and spent their time "in self-indulgence, doing nothing." They reported this last bit matter-of-factly, with curious detachment.

"Are you both from Tokyo originally?" I asked, raising my coffee cup to my lips.

Wataru slowly shook his head. "Yunosuke is, but my folks are here in Sendai. I grew up here, then went to Tokyo for high school. Stayed with my uncle. For college I did a U-turn and came back here."

"You've heard of his family," said Yunosuke, with conviction. "You like traditional sweets?"

I said that I did.

"Ever had any from Sengendo?"

The name "Sengendo" immediately brought to mind a large indigo shop curtain, a granite floor, and the faint smell of incense. The venerable *wagashi* shop actually had a waiting room for customers who traveled long distances to buy its traditional, delectable sweets. In Sendai, Sengendo was a household name.

"Of course!" I leaned forward. "Does your family run the place, Wataru?"

He was silent, as if to say he didn't want to talk about it. Sensing his reluctance, I quickly moved on. "Wow!" I said. "Well, I love their *kimishigure*.[1] My aunt likes their chestnut-paste *kanoko*[2] more, though. She teaches the piano. Sometimes she has her pupils' parents over to the house for little tea parties, and for refreshments she always has something or other from Sengendo."

---

[1] A steamed confection made from egg yolks, bean paste, rice flour, water, and sugar.

[2] Whole sweetened chestnuts in chestnut paste.

Wataru gave a polite nod and lit a Short Hope. The lock of dark hair hanging down on his forehead swung nervously.

"He doesn't get along with his parents," said Yunosuke. "That's why he moved in with me. And he never touches any kind of sweets, traditional or otherwise."

"But if you like *kimishigure*, Kyoko," put in Wataru, "I'll arrange for them to make up a big batch and send it to you. Along with some *kanoko* for your aunt."

I thanked him and laughed. He studied me with a warm smile on his lips. His gaze was so intense I could barely breathe. I looked away.

For a while we talked about music and novels. It was mostly Wataru and Yunosuke who did the talking, while I listened. I'm sure I could have pretended to know about the titles and authors they mentioned. If I'd ventured an opinion of some sort, they probably wouldn't have bothered to make sure I knew what I was talking about. When talking to college students, I often claimed familiarity with some book I had never read, or made up an opinion on a topic I had never so much as thought about. After I got home I would run out again to pick up whatever book had come up and then spend the evening cramming, marking passages with a red pen. Sometimes, on finding out that what I'd said earlier had been completely off target, I would be embarrassed to the point of tears, but even then I didn't like to admit defeat.

Around Wataru and Yunosuke I felt no inclination to display that sort of puerile pride. I wonder why not? I think I wanted to represent myself to them as a completely natural seventeen-year-old girl. Just as I had freely admitted not knowing Pachelbel's Canon, I wanted to be honest about other areas of ignorance as well. Was I afraid of them? Yes and no. On one hand, they seemed like cynics who could see straight through me; on the other, they seemed more openhearted than anyone I'd ever known. They were a strange species – youths who never talked about "the struggle" or Vietnam or Anpo. There were lots of these words that resonated among members of our generation, but Yunosuke and Wataru never mentioned them, never broached those topics.

In some ways they were like pieces of delicate glasswork, and at the same time they seemed infinitely more worldly than I could ever be. They had an air of quality and refinement, yet were somehow uncouth as well.

In the course of that long conversation, I learned that Wataru had a stepmother, that Yunosuke's father was head of a private hospital, that Yunosuke was majoring in literature despite his father's strenuous objections. How much did I talk about myself? Very little, I believe. Mostly I listened raptly to them. Their low, clear voices blended well with the baroque music. I lost track of time.

It was Yunosuke who first looked at his watch. The topic of our conversation – French writer Boris Vian, as I recall – had lagged, and a short silence ensued. Yunosuke turned to Wataru and said, "Time for me to get going."

Wataru looked at his watch, too. "Wow, it's late," he said. "Look out, Ema will be up in arms."

"Nah." Yunosuke grinned and said, "She's asleep by now." He got up. To me he said politely, "Well, Kyoko, you must excuse me. I hope you'll stay and keep Wataru company a little longer." His gentlemanly manner had a touch of languor to it.

Keeping my tone light, I said, "A date with Ema?"

He gave me a little wink. "You could say so. With a cat is more like it."

"A cat?"

"That's right. Leave her to her own devices and she dozes off. At heart, a cat."

I laughed and nodded.

Yunosuke gave Wataru a pat on the shoulder, and they said their goodbyes. He left without looking back.

As soon as he was gone, I began to feel uneasy. Wataru sat as still as a statue, eyes to the front. I racked my brains for something to say. Finally in desperation I asked, "What school does Ema go to?" Now that we were alone, talking about other people seemed a good idea. When we ran out of things to say about her, we could move on to Yunosuke. After that there were Reiko and Juri. Or my aunt, I thought.

"M. Girls' School," he said with little interest.

"She's really pretty."

"Yeah."

"In a striking way."

"I guess."

"Have they been going together long?"

"Only six months."

"How did they meet in the first place?"

"I'm not sure. She's the one who started it. Went after him, full tilt, and he got hooked."

"They make a nice couple."

"So everybody says. Picture perfect, they say."

"I think so, too."

The conversation flagged. Wataru was looking straight at me now. I fingered the handle of my empty coffee cup and blushed a little, conscious of his eyes.

"You do blush easily, don't you?"

I looked up, my face turning even redder.

"You're as red as a ripe peach," he said gently. "It shows you're genuine. It's very appealing." He was utterly calm and composed. I didn't know what to do.

"Do you like wine?" he asked. I stared at him goggle-eyed, like a country girl on her first trip to the big city. "You do, don't you?" he pressed.

"Yes, a little."

"I know a nice quiet place near here. Latin music, and the food's decent, too. Just the place to take a girl like a peach. Do you want to go?"

Instead of nodding, I did something else. I blurted out a brand-new thought: "This is all about keeping up with your friend, isn't it?"

"What do you mean?"

"I mean Yunosuke has a date with Ema, so you feel like you have to have one, too. That's it."

He gave a hearty laugh. He laughed on and on, coughed a little, and then, still laughing in the back of his throat, his eyes alight with humor, said, "What a funny, suspicious little thing you are! Well, never mind. Have it your way. My best buddy went on a date, leaving me all alone. Along comes a girl like a peach. A sweet, honest, genuine girl. I decide to spend the evening with her. You don't think much of the scenario?"

"Oh, it's okay with me," I said cheerfully. "It suits me fine, actually."

"Most girls would object if someone wanted to see them just for one evening."

"I'm not most girls," I said. "I'm not ladylike. I'm bad."

He chuckled. "Hardly. Don't bother trying to act tough, either – you're sweet just the way you are."

I turned red again. I was starting to feel like a broken traffic light. I took a deep breath and lit a cigarette, pretending I hadn't heard this.

He said with some amusement, "Don't tell me your aunt has a curfew for you?"

"There is a curfew, but my dad set it, not her."

"What time do you have to be back?"

"Seven. But she'll overlook it if I'm there by seven thirty."

I was afraid he would say something else condescending, but he let it pass. He checked his watch.

"It's five. They're open. If we left right now, we could spend a couple of hours there. What do you want to do?"

I turned straight toward him and said, enunciating so clearly that I might have been trying out for the broadcasting club, "Please take me there."

He nodded, grabbed the check, and stood up. I quickly stubbed out my cigarette and followed him out.

He took me to a wine bar five or six minutes' walk from A Cappella. It had just opened for the evening, and the interior was pleasantly cool and quiet. I sipped some white wine and listened to Astrud Gilberto sing bossa nova while Wataru talked nonstop. I don't remember anything he said. The words he spoke sank immediately into my brain and dissolved. He was as tireless as a typewriter. Words flew out of his mouth one after another, eddying around me. He laughed a great deal, ate a great deal, drank a great deal. I looked on, appalled and entranced. He was so unbelievably gorgeous, so radiant.

Not until much later did I find out the real reason he asked me out that night, and why he became so talkative in the wine bar. At the time I knew nothing. Realized nothing. I was convinced that he liked me. And already I was in love with him.

4

Meeting Wataru made my thoughts turn idly now and then to the boy I'd broken up with six months before. K, a year older than me, was an active member of a radical faction. We'd dated for half a year.

My mother and father had a strong antipathy to the student movement, so I introduced K to them as a "high achiever" from my high school. In fact he'd been expelled for his radical activities and now commuted between Sendai and Tokyo, working openly for the faction.

Being young, I found his outsider's way of thinking attractive and fell for him hard, but what he actually may have thought of me I don't know. He treated me like a toy he could stick in his pocket, taking me with him wherever he went. He didn't say very much about either the struggle or his private life. He talked about novels he'd read, poetry, and movies; he was always telling stupid jokes.

He liked to touch me, and while he talked he would keep his hand on some part of me – shoulder, arm, hand, or knee – the whole time. But he would never have done anything more than that. Not even if we'd embraced alone in the dark. Physical contact with him was strangely lacking in sexual overtones.

Once I deliberately grabbed his hand and held it to my breast. We had stopped after our date in a park where a cold rain fell steadily. In a light like the moist glow from a mercury vapor lamp, I looked up at him, my heart pounding. For the briefest second he held still. With bated breath I waited for his next move, nearly faint with apprehension.

He gave a short laugh and said, "Hey, cool it." He said it the way you'd chide a puppy. Instantly, what I'd done became something utterly stupid and regrettable.

I laughed back. That was the end of it. To banish forever the memory of what had just happened, we joked around under the umbrella and walked home talking about the weather and stuff.

We kissed only once. On the banks of Hirose River, as a freezing north wind whipped around us, he'd gingerly planted his lips on mine. It was a ridiculously childish attempt, and the thought flashed through my mind that it must be his first kiss, too. But then he said, "I'm sorry, Kyoko."

Oddly enough, as soon as he said it I knew right away what was coming. He held me close, pressing his cheek against my hair in the wild wind, and said in a low voice, "There's someone else."

I wasn't sure if I was supposed to follow this up with a barrage of questions or push him away, say goodbye, and walk on. I just stood there, feeling lost. He stood still too, for a long time. We stayed like that with our arms around each other, as if we'd turned to stone.

"She's from Tokyo," he said after a while. "She's three years older than me, and she goes to college there. I helped plan a lock-out at her campus. That's how we met."

I drew away, extricating myself from his embrace. I was in a curious frame of mind, at once sad and relieved, without a trace of anger or jealousy.

"Are you going to Tokyo?" I asked.

He nodded.

"When?"

"The day after tomorrow."

So, because he was leaving for Tokyo in a few days, he'd given me the farewell gift of a kiss. When I looked at it that way, I had a fair idea of what he'd thought of me all this time. I wasn't particularly disappointed, just lonely and depressed.

I promised to see him off at the station. His eyes widened in surprise. He was probably afraid I'd embarrass him by bursting into tears and carrying on. Had I felt like crying when the time came, I probably would have. But I had no wish to make a spectacle of myself.

Two days later I went to Sendai Station early in the morning to see K off. It was freezing cold with a powdery snow falling all around, and we laced our hands to warm them. After the express train pulled away with him on board, I shed a few tears.

At one point when we were dating, K told me he was going to get a part-time job washing dead bodies. Now it seems painfully obvious that this was a lie he cooked up to avoid seeing me. At the time I was too young to see it.

A strange rumor was circulating in the city back then to the effect that unidentified bodies from the war in Vietnam were being shipped to Japan in great secrecy for the use of medical students at Tohoku University. Part-time workers were needed to wash off blood and pus before dissections could be done. The job was said to pay ¥10,000 per body – this at a time when a typical part-time job paid around ¥1500 per day. I heard the rumor myself. Supposedly, hard-up college students and anti-war activists seeking funds for the struggle spent hours washing dead bodies, lured by the promise of easy money.

So I never doubted that K was actually engaged in this work. For a week or so after allegedly doing this he would keep his distance, saying he was "saturated with the smell of death." The whole notion of a part-time job washing the bodies of soldiers killed in Vietnam was ludicrous, but I never doubted him. Presumably he spent the time going to Tokyo to see that older coed of his.

When I tell people about K, most of them say, "Ah, so he was your first love." But my feelings for him hardly merit that kind of label. I had little understanding of love. I liked him and was greatly influenced by his ways of thinking and feeling, but that wasn't love. I would say it was merely the sort of adventure everyone has when the body matures faster than the mind can keep up.

Then was Wataru Domoto my first love? Again, I'm tempted to say no. I can't easily explain why. But I do know that the feelings I had for him were not the sort that come wrapped in flossy pale pink silk, as suggested by the words "first love." I approached him not with the softness of silk but with something much harder. Otherwise I might have been ripped to shreds.

My first invitation to Yunosuke's place, where Wataru was also living, came in mid-July, just as the rainy season was coming to an end. I caught a bus near my aunt's house and arrived at Rinnoji Temple bus stop in the Kitayama section of town at around three p.m. on a Saturday afternoon. The fierce summer sun seemed to be lurking behind the heavy clouds, ready to dispel them at any moment.

Wataru was waiting for me at the bus stop, his forehead shiny with sweat. Dressed in a close-fitting blue-gray T-shirt and chinos, he looked more grownup than ever.

He smiled when he saw my face, saying nothing, and we walked off together. Side by side we climbed the hill beside the temple, stopping along the way at a liquor store where he bought three cold Cokes and three bottles of beer, and I bought two heart-shaped almond chocolates. He asked me if I liked chocolate and I nodded. He looked at me with eyes that were wickedly clear.

It was a quiet neighborhood. Trees around the cemetery by the temple were a glorious green. The road was lined with old shops so small that there was no telling what they sold, all of them with no sign of life inside.

"It's nice here," I said. Wataru nodded. "Is Yunosuke home today?"

"Yeah, he's there."

"Not out on a date with Ema?"

"She's there too. They're listening to records."

"Oh, really?" I tried hard to sound cheerful. I didn't want him seeing my disappointment.

"She's looking forward to meeting you."

"Same here."

"Great."

In my heart I didn't want to see either of them. If I could, I'd far rather have spent the afternoon alone with Wataru. But even if I told him so, he probably wouldn't have asked them to leave. This was still only the fourth time we'd seen each other. There was no reason whatever for him to chase away his friends just so we could be alone together.

Every time I saw Wataru there was something different about him. Sometimes he'd be lively and talkative, at other times silent and thoughtful. That day he was rather reserved. As we walked along he gave short answers to my questions, and all at once I was amazed to see an old earthen wall like something from a samurai residence ahead.

"This is the landlord's house," Wataru said. "He's some kind of a distant relative on Yunosuke's father's side. A dentist. His office is over there."

I looked in the direction he was pointing, and saw at the end of the wall a one-storey building with a sign reading "Ando Dental

Clinic." So one man's residence and workplace together took up the entire block. The clinic was an ordinary construction, without any distinguishing characteristics, but the house was astonishingly imposing.

Beyond the low wall was a dense grove of trees. There was no gate; a curving line of stepping-stones beautifully tinged with hair-moss led to the entrance. It was impossible to guess from where we stood just how big the residence might be.

"Quite a mansion," I said admiringly. "I had no idea you were staying anywhere so grand."

"We don't live here. We're in the cottage out back. Follow me. There's another entrance over here. This way the people in the main house don't see us coming and going, and it's shorter, too."

He started off briskly, and I trailed after him. "How many people live in the main house?" I asked.

"The dentist and his wife and father. Other than that, there's just the housekeeper, and she doesn't live here."

"No children? Only three people in this great big house?"

"They have a son who works in Tokyo and hardly ever comes home. We don't have much to do with the family. Rarely see them. There's no need. Look, here's the way in."

Between the earthen wall and the clinic was a narrow path just wide enough to walk single file. Wataru led the way, then slipped through a small opening in the glossy green hedge. "We come and go here so often, we've made a hole," he said. "Come on through."

He held out a hand. I extended my own and lightly held on to him as I jumped through to the other side of the hedge; his hand felt dry and flimsy. A weed-grown garden opened up before us, surrounded by a grove of tall bamboo. We were now behind the main house. The garden was hardly well maintained, but amid the shrubbery was an arrangement of large, fern-shaded stones that gave it a touch of elegance. The bamboo grove and the hedge combined to keep the sun out, so there was a rich growth of moss. Up in the branches of trees swayed a number of magnificent spider webs, catching the sunlight like round silk tapestries.

A mosquito whined in my ear. I waved it away and followed Wataru along the winding path of stepping-stones. From somewhere came the strains of the Rolling Stones' "Satisfaction." It wasn't particularly loud, but neither did the music seem to be wind-borne from far away. Mick Jagger's low, raspy voice drifted through the silent garden. I looked up.

Beyond a tall clump of thick-stemmed bamboo, there suddenly appeared a small, rustic-style wooden building – a traditional teahouse. It was quite old, the paint peeling in places, the wood darkened with age. Knots in the well-weathered wood looked like the eyes of some grotesque creature.

Wataru bent down and opened the little wooden door of the crawl-in entrance. "Don't bump your head," he said. "Leave your shoes out here."

On the flat stone below the entrance, a pair of men's sneakers was lined up beside a pair of women's brown pumps. I flicked a bead of sweat from the tip of my nose and watched Wataru disappear inside as if sucked in. At the time I knew nothing about teahouses or the tea ceremony; it wasn't until much later that I understood the significance of the tiny, crawl-in entrance. Designed to accentuate the difference between the tearoom and the outside world, it forces guests to get down on their hands and knees and creep in sideways, cutting themselves off from everything outside. The entrance to Yunosuke's teahouse was to be exactly that for me, the entrance to a different world.

Many a time I slid through that entrance, each time with a sense of apprehension. I felt something nasty might be lurking inside, but I was determined to see more. Even now, twenty years on, I can remember that feeling as if it were yesterday. As I stood in front of the dark, square hole in one corner of the moldering teahouse and bent down to crawl through, I heard, like the last echo of the outside world, the rustle of bamboo in the wind.

"Come on in," Yunosuke's voice urged from inside.

After placing my shoes neatly on the stone outside, I slowly looked around. Yunosuke, wearing a singlet, was sitting with his back to the alcove. Ema Takamiya was snuggled next to him, her eyes shining as she looked at me, like a cat that had found something interesting. Behind them in the alcove was a big stereo with a neat stack of records. Mick Jagger's voice was coming from there.

I sat formally and said a greeting. Yunosuke, a short cigarette between his teeth, laughed and said, "No need to stand on ceremony here. This is just a shack, not a teahouse."

"A haunted shack," added Ema. "It's kind of nice, though, don't you think? I love it here. It's a world all its own. I know you'll love it, too."

"You two don't need introductions, do you?" said Wataru as he took out the beers and Cokes from the bag. "This is Kyoko Noma."

"Your girlfriend. I know." Ema chuckled as if this were funny. "As a matter of fact, the minute I saw her in A Cappella that time, I had a feeling she'd be your type. And I was right! It's really nice to meet you, Kyoko. I'm Ema Takamiya. Call me Ema."

"Nice to meet you, too," I said. Her chestnut hair was in the same boyish cut as before, and she was wearing a form-fitting yellow T-shirt and an olive green miniskirt. She was braless, and her breasts swelled the T-shirt to bursting, showing sweet little upturned nipples. She had such a slim waist and boyish hips that the large breasts seemed somehow out of place.

As if she'd never given this sort of thing a second thought, she jumped up, brought a bottle opener and cups from the next room, and plumped herself down next to me. "Kyoko, do you like Mick Jagger?" she asked, opening a Coke.

I said that I did. The slightly sweaty smell of her body tinged the air around me.

"It's great to relax and listen to him like this. These two guys play nothing but classical music, which is sooo boring. I'm a huge Mick Jagger fan, so I brought this record over. Here's a Coke. Or would you rather have a beer?"

"Coke's fine," I said, taking the glass she'd poured for me.

The room we were in was small, just four and a half tatami mats. The adjacent three-mat room had evidently been extensively renovated, and featured a mini-kitchen, a small toilet, built-in bookshelves and a large closet. The ceiling was high, with a central rafter and ceiling boards set at an angle. The tearoom floor was covered with a cheap gray carpet, and the only furniture was a desk. A great number of books lay heaped on the carpet and desk, neatly enough not to seem cluttered.

There were two papered windows with vertical bamboo laths. The paper was yellowed with nicotine, and had been patched with pictures cut from magazines. I went over to an open window and looked outside. A few yards away was a fence with a gate of woven bamboo, and far beyond it was the main house, built in classical *sukiya-zukuri* style. Next to the bamboo gate, stained brown from all the water it had absorbed in the rainy season, was a mossy stone lantern, surprisingly big and somehow eerie. As I watched, a sparrow flew up and perched on top of it. It chirped, ruffled its feathers, and flew off towards the garden of the main house.

"There's something creepy about that lantern, don't you think?" said Ema, looking at it over my shoulder. "I'm convinced there's a body buried under it."

"A body?"

"That's right," she said, and looked at me the way grownups look at children they want to scare. "Back I don't know when, in Meiji or Edo times – a really long time ago – somebody committed murder and buried the body under that lantern. I'll bet you anything."

"She's always going on about it," said Yunosuke dryly. "But no matter how scared it makes her, she actually likes the thing. Can't take her eyes off it."

I laughed. Wataru asked if I was too hot.

"I'm fine," I said. "It's nice here. Cool in summer and warm in winter, I bet."

"Winter here's cold," said Yunosuke, twisting around to take the record off the stereo. "Bone cold. The only heat comes from the *kotatsu* heater and the electric blanket. The only way to get through it is to curl up in the *kotatsu* and hibernate."

"Let me hibernate with you this winter," said Ema, quite seriously.

Yunosuke only gave a little laugh and didn't answer.

"I can't? No, of course not," she murmured as if to herself, reaching under her T-shirt to scratch her side. "Then poor Wataru would have no place to go."

"Don't worry, Ema," said Wataru. "If you hibernate here with Yunosuke, I'll go stay in Kyoko's room."

Hoping they couldn't see me blushing, I said, "Be my guest. I'll lay out some bedding for you in the closet so my aunt won't catch on."

"Is it cold in there?"

"A little."

"Well, if it gets too cold, I'll sleep with my arms around you. That'd be all right, wouldn't it?"

"Yes," I said, averting my eyes with a smile. Ema gave a slightly coarse-sounding laugh. I felt sweat break out on the tip of my nose.

I took a cigarette out of my shoulder bag, lit it, and restlessly blew smoke at the ceiling while furtively watching Wataru. He was toying with his beer glass and staring at a point on the rug. Then abruptly, as if he sensed me looking at him, he turned toward me. His eyes were neither cold nor warm. They were blank, as if he were looking absently at tree leaves swaying in the wind.

He's thinking of something else, I thought. *He's so close, yet so far.* I inhaled a lungful of smoke and blew it out all at once.

Still silent, Yunosuke put on the next LP, and James Brown's "It's a Man's Man's Man's World" started up. I saw Wataru drain his glass as if rather annoyed. He wiped his mouth with the back of his hand, stretched in an exaggerated way, and lit a Short Hope. Yunosuke, leaning against the stereo, calmly closed his eyes.

I don't have a clear memory of what we all talked about that afternoon. I do remember most of what I talked about with Ema, though. She was open and unreserved, and now and then she'd tell some outrageous joke, laugh loudly, and poke me in the arm. Her long pretty legs stuck out from her pleated miniskirt, and her breasts bounced as she chattered on. She was obviously a charming girl who was extremely conscious of Yunosuke and keen to win his favor.

Time passed quickly. As dusk set in, no one suggested turning on the lights. Tired of chattering, Ema fell silent. The four of us listened quietly in the gathering dusk to the record playing.

"Is Setsuko coming back this summer?" Yunosuke asked Wataru.

He looked up. "Yes."

"With that boyfriend of hers?"

"Don't know. Haven't heard anything lately."

"Araki…" mused Yunosuke.

Ema, who until then had been leaning nonchalantly against the pillar by the alcove, now said, "Araki? Who's that?"

Yunosuke muttered, "It's got nothing to do with you," and put a cigarette in his mouth.

"Why not just tell me? Who is it? Is it Wataru's sister's boyfriend?"

"That's right," Wataru himself said. "He's a grad student at the University of Tokyo. Studying law."

"Wow, impressive. Is he handsome?"

"He parts his hair on the side, and he's thin… not your type, I'm afraid."

"But he is her type?"

"She hasn't got a type. When she falls for somebody, than that's her type for the time being."

"Well, if an amazingly good-looking girl like her has fallen for him, Araki should thank his lucky stars."

I'd never heard about Wataru's sister before. He'd never spoken about his family, and I hadn't asked. I knew that the woman at the Sengendo store was not his real mother, and I'd gathered that there were other complicated circumstances.

Ema looked at me. "Kyoko, have you met her?"

"No, I haven't," I told her cheerfully. "Is she really as good-looking as all that?"

"More. You won't believe it. She looks like a movie star. Her skin is creamy, and glowing, and perfect from every angle. She's also got a stunning figure and a terrific sense of style, like she stepped out of a French movie. And to top it all off, she's brainy. Majored in foreign languages at Sophia University. Not only did she get into a hard place like that straight out of high school, but then she went on to graduate school, where she's getting top grades. To someone like her, ordinary guys must seem like hopeless jerks."

"Does she look like Wataru?"

Ema glanced at him and said "Hmm," with a show of considering the matter. "Actually they do look a lot alike. Even so, she's ten times prettier than just a female version of him. You know what I mean?"

I nodded. Wataru gave a mirthless chuckle.

"The two of them could be poster children for Sengendo. Not only that, they're tragic figures right out of a novel or something. Talk about dramatic! You've heard all about his Sengendo parents, haven't you, Kyoko?"

Aware of Wataru's presence, I shook my head. "Uh-uh."

"You haven't?" Her eyes grew wide. "Not even that they're not his real parents?"

"Leave it alone, Ema," said Yunosuke quietly. "It's no big deal. Just never mind about it."

She shrugged. "Really? A real-life story like something from a novel, and it's no big deal? I'd have thought he told her long ago."

"The reason I didn't is because it's no big deal." Wataru sat cross-legged and gave a self-deprecating laugh. "But go ahead and tell her yourself, Ema, if you want to. It's no state secret, either."

Ema looked up at Yunosuke and, seeing that he was staring silently out the window, took a big breath. "For God's sake, Yunosuke, you take everything so seriously! It drives me crazy. I mean really, what difference does it make? Things like that happen all the time."

"Who are you to say that?" he said in a low voice. "What gives you the right to say they happen all the time?"

"Well, don't bite my head off. I mean, honestly, what's so—"

With an angry gesture, Yunosuke lowered the volume on the stereo. The Rachmaninoff piano concerto receded into the distance, leaving a sound like a trapped bumblebee in the dusky air.

"Listen to me, Ema. Somebody's personal life is something no one else can possibly understand. It's not cool to pretend to know all about something you don't understand and make a joke out of it like some third-rate journalist."

"But I—"

"Quit treading all over other people's sensitivities. That's the least anyone can ask. Beyond that, fine. Do whatever you want, say whatever you want. You're perfectly free. You can take your pick of me and Wataru for all I care. Just don't go treading on people's private feelings."

"Yunosuke…"

"Hey, come on, it's all right," laughed Wataru, leaning forward and giving Yunosuke a poke on the arm to calm him down. "Don't quarrel. It's not worth it."

I thought I should comment, but had no idea what to say. I just sat there like a pigeon, blinking and looking from Wataru to Yunosuke and back again.

Wataru turned to me with a sigh. "When it comes to my family, he takes things personally. Funny thing is, we're both allergic to our families. Although why he is, I'll never know. His father's a wealthy doctor and he had a perfect childhood."

Ema sulkily asked me for a cigarette. I drew out an MF and lit it for her with a match.

Yunosuke turned the stereo volume back up. I tried to make out the expression on his face, but by now the room was too dark to see clearly.

"My grandfather was from Kyoto," began Wataru, unprompted. He spoke calmly. His voice was rather too calm, like that of someone with not long to live. "My grandfather on my real father's side, that is. He had a little confectionery shop, and when he died my father took it over. So my sister and I were both born in Kyoto. But when she was five and I was two, my dad got sick and died. My mother was always a romantic, and while she was trying to make a go of the shop on her own, she met the owner of Sengendo and fell in love. People were opposed to the match, but she'd lost her heart to him. She was willing to cut ties with her Kyoto relatives if that's what she had to do. So she closed down the shop, married him, came to Sendai. Naturally my sister and I came too. But as it turned out, my mother couldn't fit in at Sengendo. They had all kinds of old-fashioned attitudes and customs – like dumplings stuffed with sweet bean-paste, you could say. It was hard for her because until then she'd run her own place with a free hand. Her nerves just went to pieces. The owner of Sengendo, meanwhile – by which I mean her new husband, my stepfather – turned out to be a chronic skirt chaser with no shortage of skirts. In the meantime my mother was being tormented by her new father-in-law, mother-in-law, and God knows what other in-laws… It happened when I was nine. One day she was dead, just like that."

"Suicide," said Yunosuke. Low, ominous piano music from the stereo overlapped dissonantly with the word.

Wataru nodded. "That's right. Out behind the house was a big storehouse where they kept supplies, and she hanged herself from a rafter there. It was New Year's Eve. I was out flying a kite with my sister. It was a kite my mother bought us, a huge one. But for some reason the wind died down and it got stuck on the storehouse roof. We pulled and pulled but it wouldn't come down. I went and got a ladder and was climbing up to the roof when I happened to look through the little window. At first I thought she was kidding around. Hanging onto the rafter with both hands. But no. My sister started screaming like a banshee, but I stayed calm. Right then anyway. I didn't utter a word, just walked back to the main house and tugged at my stepfather's sleeve where he sat totting up sales. I led him back out to the storehouse, careful that my grandmother and grandfather wouldn't hear. After that I don't remember what happened. All I remember is my sister hiding behind a chest of drawers in a storeroom, crying her eyes out. She cried and cried. I was amazed that anybody could cry that much."

I clenched my fists in my lap. I was remembering my aunt's story about the girl who hanged herself in the shed. The stories got mixed up in my head, and for a moment I couldn't tell them apart.

Wataru scratched his neck. "My stepfather said it would be bad if word of her suicide got around, so we were put under a strict gag order. There never was a breath of gossip, either. He's careful about things like that. He paid off any employees who might have talked, and carried on in front of the rest of them like a heartbroken widower. Less than six months after the funeral, though, he took a new wife. That's my stepmother. When you go to Sengendo, there's a biddy in heavy makeup out front greeting customers, right? That's her."

I said nothing. I had no words to offer. The silence spread and the darkness felt impossibly thick and black, like India ink.

Five minutes stretched to ten. Still no one said anything. Ema got up and went to the toilet. As if on cue, the Rachmaninoff came to an end. Yunosuke took the LP off the player and solemnly put it back in its jacket.

When Ema came back, Yunosuke beckoned to her. Silently she went over and sat down, spreading out her pleated miniskirt like a fan.

"Sorry for what I said before," he whispered. "I didn't—"

"It's okay," she said. "When it's anything about Wataru, you always fly off the handle. I'm used to it by now."

"No, that's not true." He put an arm around her shoulder and pulled her close. "I was just a little stressed, that's all. Sorry." He put both arms around her and tilted her back. She shot a bashful look at me. I pretended not to see.

The twilit room was soon filled with the embarrassingly loud sound of rustling clothes.

"No, Yunosuke. Are you drunk?" said Ema, but she didn't really seem to mind. He didn't speak. Their lips met hungrily, their saliva mingled, and their breathing intensified, mixed with faint moans. Yunosuke's hand pushed up her T-shirt. She let out little cries, twisting. Her big white breasts glowed in the dimly lit interior, now like a gray pointillist painting.

I was flustered but pretended to feel nothing, looking at my hands and toying with a hangnail. Even if they started having sex right in front of me I didn't want it to faze me. I wanted Wataru to see that I wasn't an ordinary, squeamish high school girl, the kind who would give shrieks of horror and turn red every time she saw two people embrace, kiss, and be intimate.

Wataru leaned against the wall staring at a point in space. He didn't move a muscle. I thought he might be angry. *You didn't have to start making out right after I told about my mother's suicide, of all times.* This is what he seemed to want to say.

"Looks like we're in the way," I muttered. Wataru looked at me fixedly without turning his head. His eyes were so coldly appraising that I faltered. I shut my mouth.

"No, no." Ema was making small intermittent moans of protest. "They can see. They're watching."

Although I had no intention of watching or listening to them, the act of love apparently about to take place in a corner of the little teahouse was exciting to me, whether I liked it or not — and at the same time it threw me for a loop. Never in my life had a man caressed my bare breasts or stuck his hand up my skirt, nor had I ever made noises like those Ema was making now. My experience of these things was confined to the screen of the classic movie houses I often went to, where I would watch from a shabby seat.

"Oh… no…" she murmured. "They're watching."

The rustle of clothes grew louder. Mixed with it was Yunosuke's heavy breathing. I moved to the rear wall and stuck my cigarettes in my pocket, so I could get up and leave at any time. "Uh, I think maybe it's time I was going," I said.

Before Wataru could say anything, Yunosuke said huskily, in between kissing Ema on the neck, "Wataru. I'd be obliged if you took a walk, too."

For someone engaged in heavy petting it struck me as a surprisingly matter-of-fact way of speaking. After a moment, Yunosuke raised his face and looked over at Wataru. With a faint laugh he said, "You know how it is. Ema's wet."

Ema's wet. I thought over the words and flushed a deep scarlet. I felt deeply embarrassed, like someone being sexually humiliated yet breathlessly asking for more. It was that kind of feeling: a thrilling indignation.

I jumped up and dashed over to the crawl-in entrance, opened it, and slid my feet into my shoes. In my haste, one shoe went flying. I ran outside in my stocking feet, feeling the moist earth under one sole.

I could sense Wataru coming after me. Outside there was still a faint brightness in the air, but in the backyard surrounded by dense trees there was no lingering light. I turned back and saw Wataru leaving the teahouse, his figure a pale presence in the shadows.

There was no breeze, and it was terribly hot and muggy. I had no wish to hear the sounds that must be coming now from the teahouse, the sighs and whispers, the loud rustle of clothing, the animal panting. I took off across the stepping-stones as fast as I could go. The leaves in the bamboo grove were dusky and subdued, as in an ink painting. Everything was quiet.

Wataru came running after me and caught my arm tightly from behind. He pulled me so hard that I almost fell over backwards. His arms quickly pinned me. Like it or not, I was face to face with him.

"Are you angry?" he asked in a low whisper. His face was very near.

I shook my head and said, "No, why? I'm not angry."

My voice was a little shaky, and to cover it up I gave a short, strained laugh. Even on hearing that high-pitched schoolgirl titter, Wataru didn't loosen his grip on my arms. My face stiffened. I stood stock-still.

I had no idea what to do. Maybe the best thing would be to make some fatuous joke, wave goodbye, hop on the bus, go back to my aunt's house and lock myself in my room. I had a momentary vision of myself on Monday, acting out the story with gestures as I told Reiko and Juri about being in the teahouse and how two people, after hearing of their friend's mother's suicide, had suddenly started having sex.

But I couldn't move. Wataru let go of me with one hand, and used it to draw my chin closer. He wasn't rough, but neither was he gentle. Just like that he pulled my face even closer to his. It was easy to see what was coming. I felt all the perspiration in my body dry up. I looked up at him with eyes purposely wide open.

He tilted his head slightly. The movement was jerky. He was definitely going to kiss me… With perfect accuracy, his warm lips came down squarely on top of mine. I kept my mouth closed. He pressed his lips closer against mine several times, trying gently to work my mouth open, but I clenched my back teeth together and didn't respond. For a while he persisted, covering my mouth with pecking kisses before finally giving up and drawing away.

His fingers brushed my cheek, traced my lips, then lightly stroked the moist back of my neck. A mosquito started attacking my leg through my stocking.

From the teahouse came what sounded like muffled moaning. When I realized it was Ema in the throes of passion, I felt a surge of real disgust. Pretending to swipe at the mosquito, I tore myself away from Wataru's grasp. For some reason everything was now distasteful to me. I felt pathetic and foolish and unbelievably dumb.

"You don't have to keep up with him," I said, my face still stiff.

Wataru moved a step closer. "What do you mean?"

"Just because your friend is doing it with her doesn't mean you have to do it with me. Don't you see how pathetic that is? If that's all you want, there are any number of girls who'd oblige you."

I didn't actually mean it. I didn't believe Wataru had held me and kissed me out of some macho rivalry with Yunosuke. I couldn't think of him as the sort of person who would want to compete with his friend over such a thing.

He gave a sigh. It could have meant almost anything. *You're such a baby*, or, *Hell of a way for Red Rosa to talk*. I was expecting something on those lines, so when he put his arm around my shoulders and started to walk on without another word, I felt rather deflated.

The air in the mossy garden was so heavy and moist that it was hard to breathe. Wataru walked along in silence, until we came to the hedge at the corner of the yard. Then he said, "I'll see you home."

"I'm not going home. I have a date."

This wasn't true. I had nowhere else to be. I regretted having rushed home from school that Saturday, changed out of my uniform, and rushed out again. I was ashamed of naively dreaming of being invited here to be alone with Wataru, having an ordinary time whispering sweet nothings, the way people did in movies and novels.

"Kyoko." As I started to duck through the hole in the hedge, he pulled me back. I turned around. His front teeth gleamed white in the darkness. "You mustn't be angry."

"Huh?"

"Yunosuke does that with Ema all the time. It's really a…" He swallowed. "I mean, it's a perfectly natural act."

I snorted with laughter. "I know that much. Why say something that obvious?"

He clammed up. The air was sweet with the smell of summer sap.

"I like you, Kyoko," he blurted out. I felt my throat constrict with nervousness, anticipation, and uncertainty. "I like you very much."

"You do? How come?"

"Are you the kind of girl who won't let a guy say he likes her without insisting on an explanation?"

I shook my head. Air entered my constricted throat with a dry sound.

"I didn't mean anything by it. It's just…"

There was silence. I felt the inside of my nose grow hot. I didn't know why I was so agitated. Near tears, I let out my breath, and words came spilling out: "So many things have happened to me lately. So many, and in such a short time. And just now you told me all that about yourself, and then I saw those two start doing what they're doing, and… and I don't know what to think about anything."

"So many things have happened? What things?"

Again the words poured out. "I got suspended from school for what we did on the struggle committee, and I got hurt in a street demonstration… and since then I've been too scared to do anything like that ever again… I mean really, really scared. I still have nightmares. In my dreams I get cut in two by a riot police shield.

And I'm conscious the whole time. There's this sickening sound and my guts spill out on the road and I'm yelling at the top of my lungs: 'No, no! Even if you do this, I won't go home!' "

"I understand."

I looked up, sniffled, and bit my lip. "I'm sorry," I said in a small voice. "Compared to what you said before… this is kid stuff."

"You don't have to compare yourself with me. How you feel is everything."

"I didn't want to be thought of as a spoiled little girl. I didn't want to be seen as somebody who never knew what it was to be hard up – a good, well brought up young lady from an ordinary, unbroken home. Instead of doing nice, good things, I wanted to do dirty things, bad things. That's all it ever was. That must be why I get so tired. Worn out. I'm always overreaching. My head gets turned around, and then I don't know where I belong anymore."

"I like you the way you are," murmured Wataru. Through the half-light I saw him smile. All the tension left my body.

He wrapped me gently in his arms and rocked me back and forth as if comforting a child. His T-shirt gave off the smell of cigarettes and the fragrance of skin. His sweat moistened my face and chest, and my sweat moistened his shoulder.

"Can I ask you something?" I said, my face still buried in his shoulder. I felt him nod. "When your mother killed herself… who did you resent most?"

There was a long silence. Then he said only, "Who do you think?"

"Your father?"

"No."

"Then who?"

A gust of wind blew. Wataru took a deep breath. His hand on my back tensed ever so slightly. "My mother."

"Why?"

"Because she was no judge of men."

We stood for a long time in front of the gap in the hedge, our bodies pressed together, swaying. I looked up and saw, through Wataru's soft hair, the moon in a livid sky.

I found I was crying.

5

I was in the college preparatory track at school. Most of us were hoping to go to university either locally or somewhere in Tokyo. By the summer of our third and final year of high school, in desperation everyone started attending special tutoring sessions run by cram schools. Girls who usually held a copy of *The Schoolgirl's Friend* furtively under their desk, absorbed in some schlocky romance, were now studying openly for the entrance exams. The sight was somehow painful.

The only ones who continued to do nothing were me and Juri and Reiko. We spent our time pretty much as we always had. About the only difference was that the Committee for the Struggle to Abolish School Uniforms had effectively given up the ghost. This was mainly because I wasn't scheduling regular liaison meetings and debates anymore, but that wasn't all. Of the two second-year students who'd come to all the meetings, even contributing snacks, one belonged to the Revolutionary Marxist Faction and the other to their arch rival the Middle Core Faction, and they took to looking daggers at each other. As partisan politics invaded what had been a neutral movement, members began to fall away like teeth from an old comb.

One by one, they approached me with their stories. One girl cornered me behind the school, announced "I want to quit," and promptly burst into tears. Another produced a clearly made-up story about being sick, breathing so her shoulders rose and fell and looking up at me out of the corner of her eye. I nearly burst out laughing when a robust girl who never so much as caught a cold feigned a dry cough and declared that she'd begun having asthma attacks recently, but somehow I heard her out with a straight face.

I gave each of them permission to quit on the spot. That was only natural. What right did I have to force them to stay? Every time I told them to go ahead, it seemed unnatural and absurd that I should be the one in the position of saying this. I had never had any leadership skills to begin with. Me, our school's Red Rosa? Hardly.

I accepted their resignations from the committee and promised not to involve them in future. They skittered off happily like trapped rabbits let loose into a meadow.

Twenty years on, how many of them remember, I wonder. How many carry around a memory of standing in the shadowy schoolyard, which faced north and got little sun, sobbing as they confessed that they couldn't stand being a "bad girl" any longer? Perhaps I'm the only one who remembers. In the end our struggle came to nothing: two decades later, the uniform system remains firmly in place.

Reiko said she had no interest whatever either in getting into college or finding a job. "All I want to be," she told us, "is a nice little wife who stays home from morning till night. When it snows, after I send my hubbie off I'll just say 'Brr, it's cold' to myself, snuggle up by the heater, and stay like that all day, reading, if I want to. All I have to do is fix his meals and sleep in the same bed with him at night, and in exchange he'll take care of me. You want to know something? Growing old that way, without doing anything in particular, strikes me as a pretty good deal."

Every time she started up like this, Juri and I would click our tongues in disgust and call her a softy. But though we made fun of her, she refused to change her opinion.

I think now that she was right. Life does offer a surprising number of "pretty good deals," which those who mature faster than others are able to recognize and grasp. In an age when no one knew right from wrong, Reiko, who was able to set her sights on her own "pretty good deal" without being distracted by static from her friends, was probably much closer to adulthood than either me or Juri.

As long as she could read all day long, Reiko said, she'd marry anyone. She never quibbled about the meaning of marriage or pontificated about what an ideal marriage should be like. She sought a life where, catlike, she could do as she pleased. When I think how shaky her nerves must have been after her suicide attempt, how ready to crack up altogether she was, I can only bow my head in admiration of her good sense. Of the three of us she was the most muddleheaded, the weakest, and the clumsiest at living, but also the truest to herself.

My father wired a large sum of money to my aunt's bank account to cover the cost of summer cram school tuition. My aunt put on her best kimono of gray silk gauze, went with me to the counter at the school, and took care of the registration. "There's no summer vacation for students preparing for exams," she declared. "Coming to class here every day will help you pull yourself together. You've simply got to do your best, Kyoko."

In the wake of my suspension, my father had taken to phoning my aunt frequently. Her attitude to me consequently changed from one of friendliness to a colder, more businesslike authority. Still, I never attended a single session of summer school. The tuition payment, which easily topped a month's spending money for my father, was money down the drain.

I left the house early every morning untroubled by pangs of conscience, pretending to attend class. There were all sorts of places to go. I could spend the morning in the park, looking at the fountain, or read standing up for a couple of hours in a bookstore. When I got tired, I would always go to A Cappella to sip coffee and pretend to read. I knew that nothing on the page would leave any impression on me. My every nerve was focused on the door. Until Wataru opened it and came in, I would force my eyes along the lines of print.

Sometimes he would show up casually, usually with Yunosuke and Ema. While thinking wistfully how nice it would be if he came alone, I made an effort to hide my disappointment. I didn't want to be the kind of girl who makes a pest of herself by acting as though she owns a boy after one awkward kiss and hug. I was entirely natural with him. I tried to forget that he had ever said, "Kyoko, I like you." I was no baby, all set to go into raptures over a thing like that, only to come down hard later… I hoped he would get the message, but whether I succeeded, who can say.

Whenever I saw him, Wataru was dispassionate, a bit negligent and weary. He never seemed the least bit relaxed. I, of course, may have appeared the same way to him.

I hoped he would ask me out again, but all that summer he never made a second attempt to be alone with me. On the rare occasions when Ema signaled to Yunosuke with her eyes to invite him somewhere, my hopes rose, but no matter how sweetly she urged or cajoled him, Yunosuke wouldn't go off with her and leave us two in the café alone. Generally when we left, it was as a foursome.

The four of us were together as usual on the afternoon of the Tanabata Festival, one of the three major summer festivals in the Tohoku region. We were walking along a street of shops decorated with great festoons. It wasn't easy to move through the crowd four abreast, keeping together. Ema hung on tight to Yunosuke's arm, sometimes giving little shrieks, but I couldn't bring myself to take Wataru's arm. He didn't touch me, either.

When we got tired of this, we went into a cake shop called Sakharov. Ema urged me to have a chocolate cake shaped like a hedgehog. It was designed for children, with a pair of eyes and quills across the rounded back made of thinly sliced almonds. She and I each ate one while Yunosuke and Wataru looked on. "Want a taste?" I offered. Wataru said nothing for a moment, but then smiled and shook his head. He had the air of a father buying his child a cake and watching fondly as she polished it off. Not caring for the look on his face, I deliberately turned to Yunosuke and held out a sliced almond. "Try this, Yunosuke," I said. "It's delicious."

He took the thing in his fingertips and popped it in his mouth. Ema giggled. Yunosuke nodded, narrowed his eyes in pleasure, then smiled at us as if he'd already forgotten whether it was an almond or a piece of paper he'd just swallowed.

Both Yunosuke and Wataru would look at us the same way. I wondered fleetingly whether Yunosuke really was in love with Ema. She looked awfully pretty dressed in a white miniskirt, yet Yunosuke seemed not to notice. Just as Wataru didn't notice me.

As I ate the hedgehog cake, I studied the two boys across the table from us. Sitting side by side that way, they looked like a pair of Adams from a painting by Michelangelo. I was dazzled. The sight of them was so bright it hurt my eyes, yet I went on looking, afraid that if I looked away they might vanish into thin air.

I was beginning to wonder why they lived together, why they were friends at all. Sometimes they seemed like a married couple whose relationship had gone stale; the sort of couple who speak only to their children at the breakfast table, to avoid an oppressive silence. Ema and I were cast in the role of the children. Yunosuke spoke to Ema and me, and through us to Wataru. Wataru did the same. They spoke to each other directly less and less often as the days went by. They went everywhere together, yet I had the impression that without Ema and me around, they might never have opened their mouths.

But there was no sign that they hated each other or were engaged in any kind of secret feud. Of course, if they got on each other's nerves there would be no point in living together, so that was no surprise, but I don't believe I was alone in sensing a lack of the deep-rooted mutual dislike, jealousy, or suppressed derision that two men often feel.

In any case, they were constant silent companions. They gave no appearance of looking out for one another in particular, but neither did they seem to ignore each other. They were aloof, yet mutually aware of the other's presence. That's how it struck me. And I began to sense that I was incapable of coming between them.

After we'd eaten the cake and chatted for a bit, the four of us went back outside. As we walked through the noisy throng, ducking under colorful strips of paper attached to bamboo branches, I tentatively took Wataru's arm. For an instant I felt a tiny jerk in reaction, but that was all. He looked down at me with a sunny smile. I smiled back at him.

"Having fun?" he asked.

"Oh yes," I said breathlessly. My eyes were on Yunosuke and Ema far ahead of us. I could see her tugging on his arm as she looked in a boutique window. A moment later, a surge in the crowd hid their figures from us. Relief bubbled up in me. If only she would pull Yunosuke inside the shop! Then I'd be able to walk through the crush alone with Wataru.

"Tomorrow my sister's coming back from Tokyo," he said. I looked up at him. Brushing aside a strip of golden paper dangling by his forehead, he laughed a bit. "Must've been two or three days ago. I phoned her apartment in Tokyo, and she was crying. Had a fight with her boyfriend. Old enough to know better, you'd think."

"Her boyfriend? You mean Araki?"

"Yeah. They always came together before, but not this time. Do you want to meet her?"

"Your sister?

"Rather skip it?"

I shook my head. "I'd love to – of course."

"I've told her about you. She's interested in you, too."

I felt my ears turn red. Knowing that Wataru had talked about me to his sole blood relative made me happy. I repeated that I wanted to meet her. "Any time that's good for her."

"Okay. I'll talk it over with her and let you know."

Would Yunosuke be there too? Sudden doubt filled me, but I didn't ask. I didn't want Wataru to know that I saw his friend as an obstacle. *I want it to be just the two of us; I'm sick of going out with Ema and Yunosuke all the time.* When I'd had enough, I could always say so, I thought. I had a feeling it wasn't yet time.

Abruptly someone tapped me on the shoulder from behind. I turned to see the grinning figure of a plump fellow from the Sendai branch of Beheiren, the Citizen's League for Peace in Vietnam. 'T' and I had been in many a demonstration and rally together. He went back and forth between Sendai and Tokyo, and whenever he heard something big was happening somewhere, he'd rush off to help out. A shallow, show-offy kind of guy.

"Long time no see," he greeted me. "How're you doing?"

I let go of Wataru's arm. "I'm fine."

T flicked a glance at Wataru, ostentatiously removed a bit of tobacco from the tip of his tongue, and wiped it off on the back of his jeans. "I heard a rumor you jumped the fence."

"What do you mean?"

"You quit the uniform struggle committee, right? People are saying your school's on the skids without you around. You were doing so well, too – what'd you have to go and quit for? You don't come out to rallies now, either."

"Who cares? And I haven't quit the Struggle Committee, for your information."

"People will be sorry to hear you're too busy with lover boys to campaign," he said, chuckling deep in the back of his throat and giving

Wataru the once-over. "You know there are a lot of headhunters at Tonpei," he added, using the nickname of Tohoku University, "who have their eye on you."

"Come off it. What are they, talent scouts?"

"Anyway, getting back to what I said before, we're going to have folk song rallies every Saturday in Kotodai Park, building up to 10/21.[1] Bigger in scale than before. Seriously, you should come along once in a while. With 10/21 coming up, there are a lot of things we need to consult you high school students about."

"All right," I said, and dipped my head in a perfunctory bow. "See you later, then."

T gave me a disconcerted look as I spun around, took Wataru's arm and started to walk away. I could feel his eyes boring a hole in me, but I didn't look back. He had always taken an unhealthy interest in the pairings and breakups that happened in the student movement. Rumors about who'd had sex with whom in barricaded school buildings generally got started by him. Sometimes when K and I were walking innocently along like a pair of puppies, T had shouted obscene taunts from the other side of the street. The thought of the gossip he would now spread about Wataru and me made me sick to my stomach.

"You're famous," Wataru said in surprise. "And popular."

"When a girl gets involved in this sort of thing, there's always some dope around who talks like that. It's not only me. Everybody gets the same treatment," I said, laughing it off. Inside I was furious with T, but I didn't feel like telling Wataru in any detail about all the unpleasantness associated with the struggle. There were plenty of others I could rant to about that. Not Wataru. With him, there were so many other things waiting to be said.

"It's kind of embarrassing," I said honestly. "I feel like I'm always behaving so childishly in front of you."

"How so?"

---

[1] On October 21, 1967, parallel demonstrations against the presence of US troops in Vietnam were held around the world, in conjunction with a march on Washington to 'confront the war makers.'

"I can't really explain it. I just kind of suspect that to you, our efforts to get rid of uniforms, and the street demonstrations and rallies and everything, must all seem like kid stuff."

"That's not true. It's just that I don't do those things. That doesn't mean I see anything childish about people who do feel like taking action."

"Then how do you see us? As a different species? Aliens?"

"I'm envious, that's all."

The fierce summer sun beat down, stretching our shadows out on the pavement. I stopped in front of the pedestrian light and looked up at him. "Envious? Why?"

His long eyelashes shone golden in the orange sunlight. He blinked for a moment without answering. "Do you like life?"

"What do you mean? Daily life? Or being alive?"

"Being alive."

"I can't say I enjoy daily life," I said. "But I do like life. It's hard to explain. For example, on summer mornings when no one else is up yet, or winter nights when there's snow piled on the ground, or stormy days, I sometimes tell myself I love it. It's corny, I know. But I do love it, so much that my throat gets tight and I almost feel like crying. I think, *I am here, now.* And that's enough."

"Nice," he said, smiling, and looked at me. "Your life is nice, and you're nice."

It didn't sound sarcastic. The light turned green. We crossed the street without saying anything. A mother ran past us, pulling two children by the hand. When she reached the other side, she made as though she were stepping onto a podium and shouted out merrily, "We won!" Her little boy and girl echoed, "We won!" The little girl was holding a yellow balloon on the end of a string. Her mouth was smeared with chocolate.

Wataru glanced at the little girl, then smiled at no one in particular. "Unfortunately," he said, still smiling, "I don't care much for my life."

The square city hall building came into sight. In front of it was a big fountain, and its spray hung in the air like a gauzy mist, making rainbows in the light of the setting sun. We walked slowly towards it.

"Lots of people talk that way," I said, trying hard to sound adult and nonchalant. "It's textbook nihilism, that's all."

He agreed expressionlessly. "Right. A pain."

Along the way, I stole a look behind us. There was no sign of Yunosuke and Ema, and the festival crowds looked far away.

My first meeting with Setsuko Domoto came one afternoon a week later. Wataru and I met beforehand at an art supply store on a corner of Higashi Ichibancho, where he bought a sketchbook. "You like drawing?" I asked, and he gave a bashful smile. From there we were heading to a big bookstore in a building across from Sendai Station, where Setsuko was waiting. The three of us would then go and get something cold to drink on the second floor of the Sendai Hotel.

We walked in the shade of trees wherever possible, but it was the sort of day when the merciless summer sun and the high humidity made your whole body ooze sweat uncomfortably. But my spirits were high: Yunosuke had left the day before on a weeklong visit to his parents' home in Tokyo. Before he left, Ema had said she wanted to go with him, but he had flatly rejected the idea, which led to a huge fight. In the end, she stayed behind in Sendai. We hadn't heard from her since and didn't know what she might be up to.

Alone with Wataru: the thought made my heart sing. I made secret plans for the week ahead. I would meet Wataru's sister, and afterwards he and I could go for a walk along the Hirose River. The next day we might go to Aobayama, where I'd take him to all the jazz coffee shops I knew. I'd invite him to my aunt's house on the pretext of introducing him casually to her, and show him my room. We would listen to records together, eat sweets, drink tea. I could picture him laughing when he saw the empty can of peaches I used when I wanted to sneak a cigarette without my aunt knowing.

With all this in store, I talked a mile a minute. I hummed the 'Exam Student Blues,' a popular song of the day, and told him all about Juri and Reiko. I went on about how the three of us ate six times a day, including late night snacks, and were still hungry all the time. He laughed at this, his forehead shiny with sweat. Yes, he really seemed to be enjoying himself. More than ever before.

When we came to the corner by Marumitsu Department Store in front of the station, the pedestrian light turned red. I fell silent and looked across at the entrance to the first-floor bookstore. A young woman was standing outside the glass door, staring in our direction. She had on a giant straw hat and a summer dress with a sunflower print. The dress had a tiny waist and a full skirt. She stood in high-heeled white sandals, a hand on the brim of her hat, stretching up to see us. Under the hat was a wave of dark hair.

"There she is," said Wataru, a lilt in his voice. Just as I opened my mouth to say something, the beautiful girl across the street waved at us. Her long white fingers swayed in the summer light as though in slow motion. Several buses drove past. Her image came and went and came again, like duckweed floating on the water. When the buses had gone, her image was clearly restored. Radiant, blooming.

"She's pretty," I started to say, and stopped. I was literally lost for words. The light turned green, and we crossed the street side by side. In front of the bookstore's glass door, the three of us stood face to face. When Wataru introduced me to his sister, she said "How do you do?" with a smile, touched her hat, and tilted her head the way well-bred ladies do. I can't for the life of me remember whether she was wearing any makeup. My eyes were attracted not by any false eyelashes, which were all the rage back then, or elegantly thin, penciled eyebrows, but by her small, perfectly shaped doll-like face and the smile on her shining, rose-colored lips.

Bowled over, I could only go on smiling like an idiot. All at once I was miserably aware that I was a sweaty, grubby-faced, all too ordinary high school girl. I felt utterly pathetic. I wanted to run away, if I only could.

"You're a darling," said Setsuko, looking at me. Her voice was smooth and rich. "Wataru's never introduced me to a girlfriend of his before. I've been so excited, wondering what you would be like."

I thanked her. I felt that I ought to say something sparkling, but no words came. Then I saw my reflection in the glass door behind her. The french sleeves on the striped dress I was wearing made me look like a kindergarten child in costume, ready to perform a dance – or, I thought sadly, like a circus monkey. Since I wandered around outdoors every day, my skin was tanned beyond a wheat color to a dark reddish brown. To top it all off, my freshly cut hair, done in a mushroom style, was so immaculate that it looked like a black pot resting on my head.

"I was cold," said Setsuko with a slightly peevish look, taking her eyes off me and onto Wataru. "I got here too early and wandered around inside the store. The air conditioning was too strong. I have a stomachache."

"It's because you're dressed like that," said Wataru, pointing to her bare shoulders. "You might as well be wearing a swimsuit."

"It's got nothing to do with my clothes." She stood on tiptoe and put her mouth up by his ear. *I just got my period…* I caught the words clearly.

Wataru just said, "Oh," and stood looking down at her apprehensively. "Did you take something for it?"

She said yes, nodding, and rubbed her temples with her forefingers before turning to look at me as if the light were too bright. I kept quiet.

Setsuko touched Wataru on the arm. Her white fingertips settled on his wiry arm with the lightness of a butterfly and then, finding the spot to their liking, fell still. I looked away. Setsuko and Wataru walked on together like that. As though they'd forgotten all about me.

They walked together for a mere two or three seconds, yet it felt to me like two or three minutes. I will never forget the sensation of standing in the broiling sun of that summer afternoon watching their two figures recede like shadows.

Wataru stopped and looked back. "What's wrong?" he asked mildly. "Aren't we going to the hotel?"

"Yes." I put on a bright smile and caught up with them at a half-trot. Setsuko took her hand from Wataru's arm and made room for me between them. This show of consideration only made me feel worse. *Don't force yourself to be nice to me, go ahead and walk arm in arm with your brother if that's what you want.*

I was surprised to find myself already searching spitefully for flaws in her, as if any sign of latent unsavory female tendencies would help. *Just what a dirty monkey would do*, I thought derisively, disgusted with myself. I walked along with my face downturned, silent.

Setsuko studied Wataru and me and announced warmly that we made a nice couple. Wataru put an arm lightly around my shoulders, winked at his sister, and said, "She's great, isn't she?" His laugh rang out.

Standing next to Setsuko, I discovered that she was slightly taller than me. The neckline of her dress was open and her breasts stuck out like a pair of pointy hillocks. The effect was artificial, as if she were wearing a corset. She was extremely slender. The skin of her neck and bosom was unusually white. That snow-white skin hadn't so much as a freckle on it, and was so smooth that it scarcely seemed human.

She's having her period, I thought. My head swam. Among ourselves, Juri, Reiko, and I announced the arrival of our period by saying things like, "It's that time of the month," or "It's started again," or even "I've got the curse." The word "period" was altogether too raw and graphic. Why Setsuko would tell her brother such a thing in front of someone she was meeting for the first time, I didn't know. Nor could I understand why he would then worry aloud if she had taken anything for it.

Meeting Setsuko awakened something thoroughly nasty in me. From the moment I met her, I was jealous – mad with jealousy.

Once he'd introduced us, Wataru started bringing her name up in conversation all the time. He never treated her the way most boys would an older sister, bad-mouthing her, ignoring her, or using her for his own convenience. He always spoke of her respectfully, as if he looked up to her, and treated her properly. When he talked about her, his eyes shone. Whenever she came to town, he cheered up.

Until much later, I went on wondering in all seriousness if Wataru and Setsuko had ever slept together. Such doubts tormented me. Late at night when I closed my eyes, a picture would arise in my mind of the two of them embracing in that dimly lit teahouse, his lips on hers. I saw their naked bodies entwined together while they panted like Ema and Yunosuke that day. I could hear Setsuko's moans, the rustle of her clothing, the sound of Wataru's ragged breathing as his lips stroked her breast.

But in plain fact, the only time I ever saw Setsuko and Wataru in any physical contact was that summer day when I first met her. For a matter of seconds, she rested her open hand lightly on his arm. I never saw her do such a thing again, nor do I have any recollection of him putting an arm across or around her shoulders. Carried away by visions of things I had never seen in real life, I tortured myself with silly imaginings. There was something else I might have tortured myself with, had I known, but though it must have been quietly in progress even on that summer day, I was unaware.

In the tea parlor on the second floor of the Sendai Hotel, Setsuko ordered a cup of hot coffee, I ordered iced coffee, and Wataru had a beer. Revived by the hot drink, Setsuko plied me with questions. She was particularly inquisitive about the entrance exams, but didn't talk down to me in the least. She never breathed a word of patronizing advice. She was always smiling, always tactful, at pains to put me at ease.

After the better part of an hour, she suddenly closed her mouth, like a doll with a broken spring. I could almost see sharp nerve ends poking holes in the skin of her face. She sat rigid, her eyes fixed on a point in space. Procol Harum's 'A Whiter Shade of Pale' was playing. Setsuko sat for a while without moving a muscle, as if she'd forgotten all about Wataru and me.

"You okay?" Wataru asked.

She came to herself with a start, looked at him, then at me, and gave her head a little shake. "I'm fine."

"What happened? Going off into a trance like that."

She smiled weakly. "It was seeing the two of you together… made me think of Araki."

"Don't worry," said Wataru. "He'll call you one of these days."

"I hope you're right," she said, her eyes downcast, her head tilted to one side. "I'm sorry, Kyoko," she added. "I'm not in very good shape today. The next time we meet I'll be my old self again, so don't hold today against me, will you?"

"No, I – of course not," I mumbled, and stirred my empty glass with the straw.

She smiled. "Take care of Wataru."

I raised my eyes. She looked at me warmly. "He can be difficult, but speaking as a sister, I'd say he's a pretty good catch. He's never had a girlfriend before. He must be pretty serious about you."

I smiled noncommittally at this and looked at Wataru next to me. He gave a big nod. It was unreal, like a scene from a play. Unable to say anything more, I lit a cigarette. Setsuko, too, put a Seven Stars in her mouth and struck a match. The hand holding the match was trembling slightly.

After only two or three puffs, she stubbed the cigarette out. Her fingertips were a waxy white. With a face as expressionless as a Noh mask, she rose from the table like some well-bred young lady with a sudden urge to pee.

"Sorry about this, but I must be going."

"Already?" said Wataru.

"I feel a little dizzy."

A bluish stain spread in her once-rosy cheeks as we watched. If not for the bright yellow dress she was wearing, she would have looked like an invalid. Wataru was on his feet in a flash, holding out a hand to support her. Smiling, she told him she'd be fine, and put on her hat. "I'm perfectly all right. You stay here a little longer. I'm going home."

"But you don't feel good, do you? I'll take you back."

"Really, I'm okay. I'll take a taxi. But Wataru, I want to know when you're coming home. Are you planning to stay in Yunosuke's place all the summer vacation?"

Wataru sat back down and said, "If you're there, I'll come."

"When?"

"Anytime."

Setsuko said goodbye to me, telling me over and over again how happy she was to meet me. She then opened a rattan basket, took out her wallet and, removing a five hundred yen note, handed it to Wataru. He thanked her. Once again she looked back and forth from one of us to the other, smiling, before walking slowly out of the tea parlor.

Soon we could see her figure below us through the picture window. She turned and waved up at us before disappearing into one of the taxis waiting in front of the hotel.

"She hasn't slept in two or three days now," Wataru told me. "Araki wants to break up with her. There was a painful phone call last night, apparently."

"She didn't seem at all well," I said. "Maybe we shouldn't have arranged to meet her at a time like this."

"You don't need to worry about that. She really wanted to meet you. That other thing is her affair. It's got nothing to do with us."

"But what happened? Why are they breaking up?"

"Who knows? Even if she is my sister, what goes on between a man and a woman is hard for anyone else to understand."

"You didn't ask?"

"Unless she felt like talking about it to begin with, she wouldn't tell me. That's the kind of person she is."

"Oh," I said, and looked out the window. "Sometimes what goes on between a man and a woman is hard for the two of them to understand as well."

He grinned and looked at me. "You think so?"

"Yes, I do," I said with conviction. "I've never understood the first thing about myself."

"I'm beginning to figure you out."

"Liar. You couldn't possibly. If I don't understand myself, I'll be damned if I'll let anybody else."

"Silly. You're always up in arms about something. That's the main thing I've figured out about you."

Sitting there beside me in the afternoon sun, he put his arm around my shoulders and laughed so hard his body shook. I joined in, but I was aware that our laughter wasn't quite on the same track. He was still far away from me. Only that part of me where his arm lay felt hot, as if cauterized. I puffed on a cigarette till my head reeled, and went on laughing.

6

A peaceful, uneventful life is something I don't really understand. I think it may mean doing all you can to hide your premonition of coming disaster without anyone else catching on, but I'm not sure. Anyway, I wonder — is there really any such thing as a peaceful, uneventful life?

For a while things were fairly calm. At the end of summer, the cram school gave a big practice test, but I told my aunt that I'd felt sick to my stomach and had to leave partway through. She swallowed this story, so it never came out that I'd blown my summer school allowance on other things.

She telephoned my parents with the news that I had heat exhaustion. A postcard from my father soon arrived with the terse message, "Take care of yourself." My mother sent a jar of homemade pickled garlic as a remedy. I didn't want any of the stuff, so I took it to school, labeled it "Aphrodisiac," and stuck it on a shelf at the back of the homeroom. The only one who tried it for fun was Juri. During free time she tossed a whole clove in her mouth and made everyone laugh with her impression of a horny married woman.

Life was a succession of days as quiet as a becalmed sea – outwardly, anyway. The Committee for the Struggle to Abolish Uniforms was disbanded. I kept on going to school barelegged with a square-collared blouse, but this token resistance accomplished nothing.

Juri was tacitly critical of me at first for breaking up the committee, but gradually got over it. She took to opening up her sketchbook under her desk during class, doing drawing after drawing. Her first choice for college was a fine arts school in Tokyo. Now and then when we talked about our options, her comments were always vastly more detailed and constructive than mine.

"I figure I've gotta spend a year or so cramming to get in," she said flatly. "I'll go to Tokyo soon as we graduate. My parents won't like it, but too bad. I'm not taking their money anyhow. I'll crash at a friend's place at first. Get a part-time job, pay for my own food. *Of course* my friend's a girl – come on, a tomboy like me? She says come any time. She's a freshman at the fine arts school, so she'll show me around. All kinds of weird people hang out at her place, so it should be a ball."

It was Juri who suggested starting up our campaign in some other form to disrupt the approaching graduation ceremony; but whether she wasn't all that interested or because I didn't get fired up as usual, nothing came of the idea.

I went around more with Reiko. When I wasn't with Wataru and had no plans to see him, she and I would take in a movie or wander idly around the park. With her, I felt at ease. She wasn't much of a talker, and when she did say something, the ethereality of her peculiarly languorous, literary, exotic turns of phrase were a comfort to my screwed-up state of mind.

She almost never asked about my private life, but one time she did say point-blank: "Kyoko, are you a virgin?"

I gave a mechanical smile and told her suggestively, "Wouldn't you like to know," putting on a brave front. "I'll leave it to your imagination."

Juri, Reiko, and I talked to each other in language so explicit that any teacher or parent who overheard us might have had a stroke on the spot, yet none of us had ever asked the others about their virginity. I privately thought that Reiko seemed to have some sort of experience; even so, I had never asked her about it, nor did I intend to. In an age of crass outspokenness, it seems funny now that we tiptoed around this topic. But we were solicitous of each other, and despite our intense interest in sexual matters – whether or not it was just a pose – rarely broached the subject of our own experience.

"Get rid of it, honey," said Reiko in her languid way.

"Do what?"

She took a cigarette out of her uniform pocket and, with no apparent fear of being caught smoking in public, sat down on a park bench and lit up. "That's assuming you still are a virgin, of course. What I'm saying is that if you still have your virginity, you should get rid of it right away. It's nothing to defend with your life. Although I'm sure you already know that."

"Are you speaking from experience?"

"Wouldn't *you* like to know. I'll leave it to your imagination."

We sat for a while and looked at the late autumn scenery as dusk set in.

"Hey, Reiko?" I said, lazily watching the smoke she exhaled drift away. "Do you still think about wanting to die, lately?"

"All the time. But as long as you're thinking it over, you won't do it. You're only in danger when you've brooded about it 'til there's nothing left to think about anymore. I'm just barely okay, because I'm still at the stage of thinking about it."

"Do you think you'll ever completely stop thinking about it?"

"Probably someday. But I don't know. Listen to this, will you? I've thought up a new way to die. You go to a snow-covered mountain and climb it wearing your best outfit. You take three gulps of whiskey. Then you chew some Hyminal or Brovarin or something till it turns sweet in your mouth, lie down in the snow, and go to sleep. See? That way your corpse would stay pretty. That's assuming you'd be found before the spring thaw set in, of course."

"You want to look pretty even after you die?"

"Absolutely. As long as there's someone she wants to see her, a woman can't help wanting to look her best, now, can she?"

"Ah, now I get it. Your boyfriend would see how pretty you were and be filled with regret. He'd have to bear that cross for the rest of his life. That's a very Reiko-ish kind of revenge."

Her cheeks reddened slightly, and she looked at me sharply. "My, aren't we clever today!"

"Did I say something bad?"

She let her cigarette fall to the ground from between her pale fingertips and said lightly, "No, I don't really mind. It's just that you understand me so well. It's kind of discomfiting." After a beat, she said, "Anyway, tell me something, Kyoko. Have you got a new boyfriend?"

I smiled noncommittally, took one of her cigarettes, and lit it.

"I'm not about to ask you who he is, don't worry. I'm not that dense. It's just that lately, you're so much more feminine. The change is dramatic."

"Really? How so?"

"Well, let me see. How can I put it? It's as if you've got a rose-colored bomb inside you, one just waiting to explode. The least little thing might set it off and then *kaboom*, your whole body will be blown to pieces – a bomb that powerful."

"Sort of like, the Curse of Red Rosa?"

She laughed. "Don't make fun. I'm not far off, I bet."

"Not entirely."

"Sex is a kind of ritual." Reiko made this comment to no one in particular, and rubbed out her cigarette on the sole of her shoe. "And rituals have to be performed ritualistically. The sooner the better." She thrust her hands into her jacket pockets and moved her head back and forth. There was a whiff of shampoo. "Once is enough, believe me."

I pretended not to have heard this last comment.

Reiko stared emptily into space and murmured, "I loathe it."

If she hadn't said that then, I sometimes think that everything might have been different. I wanted to tell her about Wataru. Not just about him. About Yunosuke and Ema, and about Wataru's sister Setsuko, of whom I was so desperately jealous – I wanted to talk to Reiko about all of them. Why did Wataru still seem so far away after all this time? Why were he and Yunosuke always together? Why did he act toward Setsuko as if she were the light of his life?

It wasn't because I had any great faith in Reiko's powers of observation regarding other people. Nor was it because I thought her more experienced than I was in matters of the heart. I wasn't looking for answers. I just wanted someone to listen while I talked about Wataru.

If she hadn't announced in that languorous, embittered way that she loathed sex, I think I would have opened up and told her everything. Had she known about my relationship with Wataru, perhaps the problems that arose later might not have had the worst possible outcome. Had not only Reiko but Juri and other friends known, I might have listened to their ideas and taken appropriate action in time.

The name "Wataru Domoto" was on the tip of my tongue, but I swallowed it. I was still a child, overly self-conscious and as yet unaware that friends could sometimes be one's salvation. To talk about such intense things to a friend who had just confessed a deep aversion to sex seemed so awkward to me. To try and articulate my muddled, half-understood feelings to someone with sufficient experience to state with conviction that she had no liking for sex was asking too much. I was just a high school girl going on eighteen who liked to put on airs and knew little about life, someone who was all talk and no action.

"Standing on a snowy mountain, chewing Brovarin till the taste turns sweet... Maybe that's it," I murmured.

Reiko's eyes widened with surprise as she turned to look at me. "Stop it, Kyoko. That kind of talk doesn't suit you one bit."

"No? Why not?"

"Before you do a thing like that, you've got to set off that rose-colored bomb." She giggled. "Do it in a big way, knock your lord and master right off his feet. Not such a bad idea."

Not a bad idea at all, I agreed.

That November I turned eighteen. My birthday fell on a Sunday. In the morning my parents called to wish me happy birthday, and a drawing of a bird came in the mail from my sister. It looked a little like the Java sparrow she'd had to leave behind in Sendai, and she'd written on the card, "This is Petey."

My parents, who had not a doubt in the world that I was hard at work preparing for my entrance exams, sounded warm and loving on the phone. Fortunately, I had managed to squeak by with decent grades last quarter; otherwise there was a good chance that they would have come straight to Sendai and locked me in my room. In that way, I was a careful strategist. There would be plenty of time to argue later on, if it came to that. In the meantime, part of me believed it was my filial duty to keep them in the dark for as long as I possibly could. Anyway, I had no idea what lay ahead, and I didn't want to think about it. I went on chirping stupidly into the receiver every time they called.

My aunt's piano pupils were giving a recital that day, and she would be out all afternoon. The recital would end at five. Afterwards she had to attend a dinner hosted by the families of her pupils, which left her feeling pretty guilty toward me. Having taken on the responsibility of providing a home for me during this year, she felt it her duty to cook me a proper birthday dinner; not to do so was a violation of her strict, old-fashioned principles. She apologized profusely, and suggested that I accompany her to the dinner.

I politely declined, saying that I wanted to stay at home as I had plenty of studying to do. She complimented me on my dedication and declared enthusiastically that all my hard work was sure to be rewarded with first-round success. I told her proudly that she could count on me, and went back to my room. She changed into her best kimono, called a taxi, and left the house in high spirits.

After she was gone, I filled the tank of my kerosene stove, opened the window and cleaned my room. It was a cloudy, freezing day. I could see Mogu lying curled in a ball, asleep in the shed.

When I'd finished cleaning up, I turned on the stove, took off the fuzzy gray sweater I'd been wearing, and changed into a blouse with crisscross orange stripes and a white mohair cardigan. I inspected myself again and again in front of the mirror, checking to see that my stockings had no runs and brushing my hair carefully.

I made tea in the kitchen and laid a white napkin across a dish before filling it with cookies. I nibbled on a cookie, then took the brandy my aunt sometimes drank when she couldn't sleep and decanted it into a small glass container. Just then the doorbell rang. I rushed to the kitchen and checked in the cheap mirror on the wall that there were no cookie crumbs stuck to my teeth before running to the door.

Through the diamond-shaped glass panels I could see a dark silhouette. I knew perfectly well who it was, but called out innocently, "Yes?" A low, resonant voice responded, "It's Wataru."

This was the first time I had ever invited him to my aunt's house. Once when she and I were out shopping in a department store we had run into Wataru and Yunosuke, and I had introduced them to her; but the idea that I might invite Wataru to her house and celebrate my birthday there alone with him surely never crossed her mind.

After we'd chatted briefly with them in the department store and gone our separate ways, my aunt had said, "His father runs Sengendo? Wherever did you meet him, Kyoko?" Her tone was disapproving. "For someone who spends all her time studying, you certainly do get around."

I instantly replied, "It was in the university library. I dropped my eraser on the floor, and he was sitting next to me, so he picked it up for me. Then he dropped his pencil, and I picked that up for him."

"Oh, you met him in the *library*," she'd said, sounding relieved. As if she believed that any man I met there must be intellectual, cultured and harmless. And yes, Wataru was all of those things. In that sense, she was right.

When I opened the door, Wataru smiled at me. He was wearing a heavy black turtleneck with a long white muffler around his neck. "Happy birthday," he said with a flourish, and presented me with a small bouquet of roses.

There was a card sticking out on which he had written in a felt pen, in English block letters, "HAPPY BIRTHDAY MY DEAR KYOKO." My eyes went over the "MY DEAR" part several times, hoping the words held some special significance. I said "Thank you." The moment I said it, I felt a hot rush of emotion and threw my arms around his neck.

He gave a stifled laugh. "Hey, the neighbors are watching."

"It's all right." Stung with embarrassment, I drew away from him. "My aunt won't be back 'til eight."

"Makes me sound like an undercover lover," he joked, coming into the house. I showed him into my room next to the entrance and dashed off to the kitchen to get a vase for the flowers. My heart was throbbing painfully. Wataru was here, in this house. In my room. The thought tightened my chest and set me trembling with nervousness.

I felt as if he would see through me, could picture how every day I sat in that room and thought of him with an anguish so keen it was indecent. Muddled thoughts of him permeated the room, its walls and floor and ceiling. Wouldn't specks of them emerge and fly at him now as he sat there, and drive him away?

Without realizing it I buttoned up my white cardigan and wrapped my arms around myself. The house was silent. No sound came from my room. I swiftly arranged the roses in a vase, then buried my face in them. The chill petals cooled my flushed cheeks. In the sink, water dripped from the faucet, its washer worn out. I counted ten drops before lifting my face.

I carried the vase of roses back to my room, to find Wataru standing by the open bay window, looking out. He turned around and smiled. I smiled back.

"Nice room," he said. "Plus you've got a great view here."

"My aunt has always liked gardening. She put this lawn in herself, a long time ago. The dog kind of wrecks it, though."

Mogu came running up out of nowhere and gave a loud howl. Wataru asked me his name, then called "Mogu, Mogu," holding his hand out. Mogu wagged his tail furiously, dashed off and ran in circles, then came back again. We burst into laughter.

With the lights off, the only source of light in the room was the dim red glow of the kerosene stove; everywhere else, soft darkness seeped in. I closed the window and moved away from him.

"You can smoke if you want," I said. "There aren't any ashtrays, though. My aunt doesn't smoke and she doesn't have any visitors who do, either. So here, use this instead." I took out the empty can of peaches I always used when I wanted to sneak a cigarette and set it on the table. Wataru smiled in amusement. I sat down on the chair by my desk, and he sat on the bed. The freshly washed dark red bedspread made soft wrinkles under him.

For a while we talked about neutral topics, like the books in my bookshelf, Mogu, my aunt's piano pupils, her personality, and so on. I did most of the talking. He listened well, adding appropriate comments at all the appropriate places; where I hoped he would laugh, he obliged by laughing out loud, and where I hoped for a sensitive response, he said something quite discerning.

When we had finished this ceremonial chitchat, I turned on the stereo and played a record by the Bee Gees. Strains of 'World' filled the room. I poured tea in the teacups I'd gotten out beforehand and set them on the table with the cookies. Wataru didn't touch the cookies, but he drank two cups of brandy-laced tea with obvious enjoyment.

"I thought a lot about what to get you for a present." He said this as he put a cigarette in his mouth, after finishing his second cup of tea. "Some kind of accessory, or a sweater, or maybe something to eat, even. I don't know how many trips to the department store I made in the last ten days. I asked Yunosuke and Ema what they thought, but you know them. They just say the first thing that pops into their mind. No help at all."

I laughed. At his feet was a square, flat bag. I had a feeling I knew what was inside. He took a slow drag on his cigarette and then smiled, exhaling smoke. "In the end I got you an LP. It's my favorite recording. I've never given it to anyone before. I hope you like it."

Inside the bag he handed me, an LP was beautifully tied in a red ribbon. I drew it out with a cry of delight, carefully slipped the ribbon off and looked at the jacket. The record was Tchaikovsky's Symphony No. 6 in B minor, the 'Pathétique.' The Leningrad Philharmonic Orchestra, conducted by Mravinsky…

I don't know quite how to put what I felt at that moment. Disappointment? Something close to that, perhaps. He had not given me the music we'd heard when we first met, Pachelbel's Canon, or anything by Bach or Rachmaninoff, or any more popular stuff like the Supremes, the Rolling Stones or the Beatles. He had given me the Pathétique.

The title made me think for some reason of a colorless field buried in snow. Careful to keep my smile from freezing on my face, I looked at the dark, gloomy picture on the jacket. It reminded me of Utrillo's dingy snowscapes.

"You don't like Tchaikovsky?" he asked anxiously.

Quickly I recovered. "Yes, I do! I love him. This is great. Thank you. Is it okay if I play it right now?"

"Of course."

I plopped down in front of the stereo and traded the Bee Gees for Tchaikovsky. The room had warmed up, and the flame in the kerosene stove blazed brightly. Steam rose steadily from the kettle on the stove, and the windows were covered in a veil of condensation.

As I listened, I sat on the floor and read the notes on the record jacket. The words didn't penetrate. I could feel Wataru's eyes on me from where he sat on the bed. I didn't move a muscle, pretending to be absorbed in the text.

I had never heard the Pathétique. It sounded sadder to me than the saddest music I'd ever heard in all my life. For a long time we listened in silence to its poignant strains. Once in a while, the sound of Mogu growling at something or other came through breaks in the music. He didn't howl, he only growled.

"Kyoko," Wataru said huskily. I looked up. "Come over here." I said nothing. He said again, "Come on over here. Sit by me."

I went over and sat down next to him on the bed. The bedsprings squeaked lightly under our combined weight. His arm crept around my shoulders. I felt an intense sadness.

"This music makes me want to cry," I said. "Why do you like it?"

"I don't know," he murmured. "It's calming."

"Oh."

"Sorry." The arm around my shoulders tightened a little, and he patted me as if offering comfort. "I guess you don't like it much."

"Oh, I do," I said emphatically. "I just think it's a tiny bit *too* sad, that's all."

He touched his forehead to mine, as though feeling for a fever, and we stayed that way for a while. "I wanted you to hear it. I like just knowing you're listening to this."

I lifted my face timidly. I was swept by the urge to cry, but no tears came. My mouth opened. "Wataru," I said.

"Mm?"

"What is it that's bothering you so much?"

With his usual air of humoring a child, he put on a light, indulgent smile, as if to say everything was all right. "Do I look bothered by something?"

"Yes, you do," I said plainly. "You always do. Even when you're laughing, or talking a mile a minute about something, or eating, or drinking, you always look like you're thinking about something else. You're always far away. I feel like however I try to hold onto you, you go on drifting someplace further and further away from me. The more I'm with you, the more I feel that way. It's as if you'd left half of you in another world."

Perhaps because I had resisted saying anything about this for so long, I began to talk with appalling frankness. I told him exactly how he appeared to me. Having to speak in abstractions was exasperating, but even so, without mentioning Yunosuke or Setsuko by name, I did my best to convey the invisible membrane that I sensed surrounding him.

I can't remember how he looked as I said these things. All I could see was his eyes moisten and lose their luster, turning into dark pools of water. Nevertheless, I couldn't stop the torrent of words from pouring out.

Before I knew it, the record had finished. I felt my words absorbing into the still air in the room, and closed my mouth. The kettle on the stove was giving off steam with a light whistle. Though it was only a little after five, outside it was quite dark.

I apologized. "I don't even know what I'm saying. Pay no attention to me."

I reached out to the lace-covered table and drank the last of my tea. It was stone cold and tasted only of the lemon and sugar sludge at the bottom of the cup.

I replaced the teacup, and all at once Wataru took hold of me so tightly that it hurt. In my surprise I knocked the teacup over. He didn't loosen his grip.

His body felt as hard as concrete. Why did I try to resist? I had half-anticipated this kind of roughness from him, yet I put my hands against his firm chest and tried to shove him back. He wouldn't budge. The next moment, I lay toppled over on the bed.

His face was directly above mine. He looked down at my flushed face almost in anger. His dry lips were before my eyes, and he let out an agonized groan. For an instant he closed his eyes and took a deep breath. When he opened them again his mouth came down to cover mine, and my arms reached for him, up around his neck.

Even now I can remember the exact movements of his hands as he tried to undo my bra. He inserted a hand under the mohair cardigan and pressed his fingers against my vertebrae like a back brace, searching for the hooks. The hooks wouldn't cooperate. I arched my body awkwardly to try to make them come undone, and his moist hand swam clumsily around in the small space under my back, but try as he would, he couldn't undo those hooks.

I felt awkward and embarrassed, and twisted to one side. He gave up on the hooks and felt my breast through the blouse. Buttons came undone. Roughly he shoved up my bra to expose my breasts, then crouching on all fours, looked steadily down at me. His nostrils twitched. I felt faint, like a girl in a dressing room who'd collapsed in her underwear from anemia.

He closed his eyes. Clenched his jaw. Through his gritted teeth burst an odd, sad groan. Then with an animal sound he straddled me. He ripped off my blouse. His mouth was everywhere on my skin, caressing, biting, and with both hands he reached to pull up my skirt.

The bedsprings squeaked loudly. In confusion I let out a small scream. He seemed clueless: I sensed in him the frantic misery of a boy who, unable to remember for the life of him what he's after, plows determinedly on.

His soft hair covered my eyes as I thought instinctively, *He's never made love to a woman before.* An image of Setsuko rose in my mind. *Maybe he can't make love to anyone but her.* That's what I thought.

When his hands tugged on my panties, I cried "Stop it!", my eyes filling with quick tears. He stopped moving in surprise. In the red glow of the stove, our grotesque postures were outlined on the wall like a shadow pantomime.

Lying face up, I bit my lip. The back of my nose felt hot, and tears spilled out. Why I was crying I wasn't sure. Thoughts of Setsuko filled my mind. My suspicion that she and Wataru were sexually involved came to a head.

"It's Setsuko, isn't it?" I cried, like a fretful child. "*She's* what bothers you so much. You can't love anyone but her. That's it, isn't it?"

"What the hell are you talking about?" he said in a flat voice.

"I understand. I know you love her. Not as a sister but as a woman. I could tell it the first time I ever met her."

For a long time, he said nothing. Gently he drew the mohair cardigan around me to cover me up, then pulled away with a distracted air.

I sniffled and said, "It's all right. Even if it's true, I don't care. I don't care one bit. These things happen. It's not unusual for a brother and sister who shared a painful childhood to fall in love."

"That's crap," he said harshly. "You've got it completely wrong. I'm not in love with my sister."

I sat up on the bed. "Then tell me. Who are you in love with? Answer me that."

It's probably just as well that I didn't hear his answer right then. I looked hard at him. He returned my gaze, his mouth moved as if on the point of speaking, and then the phone in the living room rang. In the hush it sounded with loud insistence. I pulled my skirt down and stood up.

I didn't have the slightest inclination to answer it, but as my sense of reality slowly, it dawned on me that it might be my aunt, and I panicked. Maybe something had happened; maybe she was calling to say she didn't have to go to the dinner after all and was on her way back. In that case I must send Wataru packing, wash the teacups and put them away. Erase all trace of his presence. Starting now.

I wanted to stay with him 'til nightfall, just the way we were. I didn't care who he loved. I regretted having asked such a stupid question. I didn't want to lose him. It came to me with sudden, fierce clarity how much I loved him and wanted him. How he made love to me didn't matter in the least. Better by far to be pawed clumsily than to be ignored.

"Gotta answer the phone," I mumbled. I slipped my cardigan over my shoulders and readjusted my bra. If she was coming home, I'd go out somewhere with Wataru, I thought. My mind clung to that idea.

The phone rang and rang. I flew out of the room and down the hall to the living room. As I picked up the receiver, my cardigan slipped from my shoulders to the floor. Standing there in my underwear, I said, "Hello?"

There was the clink of a coin falling into place. "Is this the Nomas' house?"

It was a dreadfully flat, cold voice. I reached for my sweater, picked it up and clutched it in a ball at my chest. I didn't have to ask whose voice this was.

Yunosuke gave a perfunctory laugh, then said, "Today's your birthday, huh. Happy birthday, Kyoko."

"Thanks," I replied.

"How does it feel to be eighteen?"

"It feels like, gee, I'm eighteen, that's all." Aware that I was half naked, I laughed artificially. "When I was in grade school, I figured I'd die when I turned twenty. That gives me two more years."

"When you're twenty, you'll think you'll die at thirty. And probably when you turn thirty, you'll think what the hell, might as well go on living."

"No doubt." I gave a shrill laugh.

There was a brief silence. Yunosuke cleared his throat in a strained way. "Is Wataru there?"

"Yes, he is."

"Would you mind putting him on? Something's happened to Setsuko."

"What is it?"

A taut silence. "She's in the hospital."

"What?"

"Wataru got a telegram just now from Araki. It looks like... attempted suicide."

I mumbled something and threw down the receiver, then ran back down the hallway and into my room. Wataru was sitting hunched over on my bed like a great dark shadow. I told him Setsuko was in the hospital, and he jumped up and tore out of the room.

After talking to Yunosuke, he asked me if he could make a long-distance call to Tokyo. There was no reason to say no. He dialed the number of the hospital that Yunosuke had given him, had Araki paged, and talked to him for a long time. The living room was unheated, and the longer I stood there the colder I became. Wataru said nothing but "Yes" and "I see." The words piled up in the chilly room like ice cubes.

He hung up and turned to face me. The corner of his mouth twitched with a smile like a spasm. "I'm so sorry, Kyoko."

"You're leaving, aren't you," I said, repressing my resentment. "You're going to Tokyo, right?"

"No," he said. "She's got Araki with her, and her condition has stabilized anyway."

Why did she do it? How? I didn't ask. In the freezing living room, Wataru gently drew me close. "I'm sorry," he said again. "I have to go back to Kitayama now."

"It's okay," I said. "Don't worry about me."

"We'll celebrate your birthday another time. I'll take you to a nice restaurant or somewhere."

"Right," I said, and pulled away.

After he was gone I washed out the teacups in the kitchen, wiped them with a towel, and put them back on the shelf. I straightened the bedspread in my room, opened the window to clear out the smell of smoke, then went into the yard and fed Mogu. He gobbled down a mixture of rice, chicken gizzards and miso soup, then I tied him in the shed and went back to my room.

With the lights off, I smoked a cigarette and listened to the record Wataru had given me. After listening to each side twice, I crawled under the covers and cried a little.

7

At the end of December Setsuko came back to Sendai, accompanied by her ex-boyfriend Araki. It had been his idea that she return home to recuperate, and she had agreed, effectively ending their relationship.

Wataru and I went to the station to meet them. Araki was carrying four items of luggage, including an overnight bag filled to bursting, and some paper bags. She had only a small clutch bag. We deposited her things in the baggage storage office and went to a nearby coffee shop.

This was, I think, the fourth time I had seen Setsuko. She gave me a hollow smile and introduced the guy with her as "my friend Mr. Araki."

He was wearing black-framed glasses. He turned to me and said with a slight tilt of his head, "How do you do." His features were even, but to me there was something a bit shady about him. It might have had to do with what he was wearing: a navy blue suit, that I guessed was his one good one. His dull hair was parted neatly on one side. If not for the dandruff, he might have looked the part of a go-getter salesman.

Actually, depending on how you looked at it, the slight shadiness might have been an asset. Maybe that was why Setsuko had fallen for him. Why anyone with her brains would go for this guy – let alone attempt suicide over him – was hard to imagine. He looked incapable of anything romantic. The moment he murmured something loving in your ear he'd probably panic and add a quick disclaimer, afraid of being held to a commitment.

Setsuko turned to Araki and said, "Well, it's a relief to be here." Then she addressed me: "Kyoko, you've probably already heard this from Wataru, but Araki and I have decided to split up."

Araki dragged on a cigarette, frowning slightly. He didn't look as if her matter-of-fact explanation had upset him, but rather as if he was anxious not to rehash the topic.

"Yes, what a relief!" she said again in an upbeat way. "I feel a lot more relaxed here in Sendai. If I can just take it easy here 'til spring, I'm sure I'll get better."

"You'll get well, I know you will," said Araki quietly. It was like listening to dialogue from a B movie. As Wataru and I looked on, he took Setsuko's hand lightly in his, eyes averted, and said, "You have to, for my sake."

She nodded and looked up at him with a tight smile.

Wataru had said little about his sister's suicide attempt, but I knew the bare facts: she'd taken a large dose of sleeping pills, filled the dishpan in her sink with water, and slit her wrists. It was Araki who found her. He'd received that same day a letter from her that sounded ominously like a farewell note, and had rushed over.

Setsuko's attempt on her life wasn't an act of impulsive despair because he played around or because her love was unrequited. Rather, she'd come to the considered conclusion that her feelings and his were on different tracks, and would never coincide. And now that I'd met him, I suspected she was right. Something about him would frustrate any woman he was involved with, it seemed to me.

I dropped my eyes to Setsuko's wrists, hidden in the sleeves of a fluffy white sweater. The scars didn't show. All I could see were her hands, whiter than the sweater.

The four of us chatted for the better part of an hour before leaving the café. Grimy traces of the previous day's snowfall lingered here and there in the streets, giving the city a bedraggled look.

We went back to the station and retrieved Setsuko's luggage. With nothing left to do, Araki said to no one in particular, "Okay, then. I'll be off."

"Too bad you couldn't stay the night," said Wataru politely. "Sorry to see you head straight back."

Araki smiled at him. "It's okay," he said. "My job was to deliver your sister here safe and sound."

"I'm fine now," said Setsuko with forced brightness. "Thanks so much for all your trouble. I'm really glad you came with me."

Araki smiled at her awkwardly, his cool eyes crinkling behind his glasses. There was still a little time before his express train was scheduled to leave. Wataru and I left them alone, carrying Setsuko's bags between us.

We left the wooden station building, and when we reached the taxi stand I turned to look back. They stood facing each other at the ticket gate, looking into each other's eyes. She said something; he said something. She raised the collar of her warm striped coat and took a step towards him. He bent down and kissed her on the cheek. One arm circled her lightly. She buried her face in his coat and stood unmoving while passengers went to and fro around them, giving them sidelong looks. He patted her lightly on the back before quietly drawing away. I couldn't see her expression, but he clearly looked relieved. It was the look of someone who had stuck a kitten in a basket and left it on a doorstep somewhere.

He took his ticket out of his pocket, made a slight bow, and walked off. Even after Araki had gone, she remained motionless by the gate. A very long time went by and we waited patiently. Then the departure bell for his train rang out, and she promptly turned on her heel and came towards us. She wasn't crying. Her face was empty. When she saw Wataru, she softened.

"He's gone."

He nodded. "It's okay."

"Yes," she said, and turned to me with a fixed smile.

"You'll be fine," I said.

She frowned and looked as if she might cry, but didn't. "Kyoko," she said suddenly, "let's go out drinking, the three of us. You drink, don't you?"

I said yes. So the three of us, laden with bags as we were, piled into a taxi, went to a jazz café I knew, and drank Coke highballs. Because I felt a bit decadent drinking alcohol in the middle of the day, or because I was afraid that Setsuko, having broken up with Araki, would now get even closer to Wataru, I downed two highballs, with no discernible effect.

Mal Waldron's 'Left Alone' was playing. The only other customers were a quartet of college students I recognized from anti-war demonstrations.

"Really, this is such a relief," Setsuko kept saying, like a broken tape recorder. "Now I can start life over. After I finish grad school,

I think I'll come back here to live. Find a husband, someone who'd be willing to take the family name and help carry on the business. You wouldn't do it if they got on their knees and begged you, would you, Wataru? So I might as well, right? It should even do me good. Being the owner of an old-style confectionery shop would suit me very well, actually. I never used to think so, but lately I've started to change my mind. Really and truly, I have." Whether she was drunk or her frayed nerves had put her in a manic mood, I don't know, but she kept up a constant stream of chatter, nodding to herself, posing questions and answering them.

We each ordered a third highball, and just as Wataru was asking a waiter for two packs of Short Hope, Setsuko suddenly fell silent. She let out a deep breath and closed her eyes. The corners of her mouth drooped. Tears ran down her cheeks. She wept silently for a time, then gave a wan smile. I pretended not to notice, applying myself to my drink when it arrived.

Without wiping her tears away, she said, "Wataru, do you think you'll ever go back to Sengendo?"

"No," he said flatly.

"All right," she said. "I see. What about your living arrangements with Yunosuke? Are they permanent?"

"Who knows."

"He's got Ema, hasn't he? You might be in the way."

"Could be."

"And that place is so dark."

"I know."

"You should find yourself a nice, sunny place to live."

"When the time comes, I'll let you know."

"Find yourself a nice, sunny apartment and live there with Kyoko. That's the thing to do."

I looked at her. Without a glance at me, she stared vacantly around the dim, smoke-filled room. Her fawnlike eyes filled again with tears.

"When will I be my old self again?"

"Don't think about it," Wataru said quietly. "Don't think about anything now."

"Right," she said, and picked up her drink, her hand looking pathetically frail. A cheap ring on her middle finger clinked against the glass.

Why, I couldn't say, but at that moment I suddenly liked Setsuko. I felt an overpowering sympathy for her. Though aware that the feeling could turn in the blink of an eye to hate or jealousy, I felt able to accept her.

I turned to her and started telling rather lame jokes, trying to make her laugh. At first puzzled by this sudden wisecracking, she seemed to get what I was doing, and responded with a tactful burst of laughter.

When we left the café, it was evening. Wataru hailed a taxi for his sister, piled her things on the seat, and promised to give her a call the next day. "Come on over tomorrow," he said. "You and Kyoko. The four of us will have some fun."

"Okay," she said, and disappeared inside the taxi.

The next day he called Sengendo, but Setsuko was in bed with a fever, and plans for us to get together fell through. This low-grade fever of hers hung on for quite a while. By the time she recovered it was January, long after Wataru and I had made our attempt at what Reiko called "the ritual." How Setsuko and I got along after that, I can scarcely remember. I do know that she was forever popping up between him and me with nerves as delicate as glasswork, trying hard to seem in control. The three of us – sometimes accompanied by Ema or Yunosuke or both – would often drink Coke highballs together. Now and then we went to A Cappella. Setsuko was fond of the Brandenburg concertos, and requested them every time.

That's about all I can remember. I have no clear memory of what she said or did, or how she related to me. What was seared in my mind was the image of the two of them lying naked in each other's arms. Even after I knew it to be a delusion, it still wouldn't go away. It's strange, but even after twenty years, when I try to remember Setsuko all I can see is her and Wataru locked in a passionate embrace. Like an old snapshot in an album I can't throw away, that image continues to torment and fascinate me.

The year 1966 ended, bringing in its wake a wild, gray storm. The times themselves rocked and swelled like an ocean. The nationwide student rebellion spread from college campuses to high schools, where it became deeply entrenched, causing a steady stream of teen arrests. In Sendai alone, there were anti-war demonstrations nearly every day. The air resounded with protesters' angry shouts, and handbills littered the streets. On any chilly corner all someone had to do was pick up a guitar, and a crowd of students would materialize out of thin air and start singing anti-war songs. The police would come, and after a skirmish would drive them off, but they would soon reappear somewhere else and sing the same songs again. Day after day, newspapers printed the number of students arrested or injured in demonstrations, and TV news shows featured in-depth reports on conditions at campuses beset by strife.

I watched the news from the warmth and safety of my aunt's cozy living room.

Wataru was all I cared about.

The events of one day in early February are still fresh in my mind. Snow began falling the previous afternoon and piled up until it set a record in Sendai. After a night of little or no sleep, I got up in the morning and poked around my room for a while before braving the living room. My father, sitting across from my aunt, gave me a hard look.

The night before, he'd slapped me. I had figured it was a matter of time before all my lies – about summer and winter cram school, taking practice tests, studying hard every day – caught up with me, and I was right. First my aunt found out that I'd taken all the exam guides, application forms, and college catalogs my father had so faithfully sent me, and burned them in the backyard. This upset her so much that she called him to report it, and everything started to unravel. His suspicions aroused, my father got in touch with the cram school and my homeroom teacher. The cram school attested that while my name was on their books, I had never taken any of the practice tests they organized; my homeroom teacher stated that I continually left school early, came late, or was absent, and showed no sign of ever studying.

"Without your school uniform on, where do you think you're off to first thing in the morning, young lady?" demanded my father.

"There won't be any classes today," I said. "Not in this snow." As a makeshift breakfast, I pocketed two tangerines from the table and started to leave. In the course of a sleepless night I'd made up my mind to apologize and ask for his understanding… but I was unable to say a word of the speech I had rehearsed.

"Hold it," he said. His voice sounded weary.

I stopped and turned back.

"Sit down. We need to talk."

My aunt looked up at me fretfully, as if imploring me to be a good girl and do as he said. I stood motionless for a moment, trying to decide if I should say the things going through my mind: *I don't want to hear anything more, I have nothing to say to you. If I want to go to college I'll pay my own way, so just leave me alone.* But before I knew it, I was sitting down beside him.

"This is as bad as it gets," he said solemnly, his arms crossed. "It means I brought up my daughter to be a common liar, someone who doesn't give a damn. I'm this close to telling you to go straight to hell for all I care."

I remained silent.

My father cleared his throat. "But I can't do that. So let me ask you one thing. Do you have any desire to go to college?"

"I don't know," I said.

He looked straight at me. "Yes or no? Which is it?"

"You want me to say yes, is that it?" My aunt wriggled closer and pinched my knee under the *kotatsu* quilt. I brushed her hand aside and said, "If you pay, I don't mind going." I braced myself for another slap, but instead he looked away, a blue vein throbbing at his temple.

"If you think you can pass the entrance exam after a year of studying," he said, "I'm willing to pay. But…"

I cut him off with a scornful laugh. "Forget it, Dad. I know what you're going to say. You want me to live with you in Tokyo and go to a cram school there, right? Well, I'll tell you one thing right now: I don't want to go back to Tokyo yet, I want to stay here in Sendai."

"You mean go to cram school here? Stay on another year in your aunt's house, make more trouble for her?"

"It's no trouble," said my aunt feebly. My father wasn't listening.

"Do you have any idea what you've put her through this past year already? As if asking her to take on a third-year high school student preparing for entrance exams wasn't imposition enough, you've gone around disrupting your school like some kind of hoodlum, spouting nonsense about politics and revolution – things about which you know absolutely nothing – causing trouble for her and dragging her name through the mud. Aren't you ashamed?"

"When did I drag her name through the mud?" I protested. "I never dragged anybody's name through the mud. This is *my* problem."

"You are an absolute scandal."

"If that's what you think, fine."

"What kind of a kick do you get out of lying to your mother and me? Does being a political activist mean that much to you?"

"I'm not a real activist. The real thing's way more intense. People go all out, stake their lives on it. What I've done is different. How many times do I have to tell you anyway? It's *my* problem. You'll never understand. Somebody like you who's just a company man, bowing and scraping at the office and letting it take over your life, what would you know?"

"Get out," said my father softly. It was almost a moan, so low that I barely heard it. I shut my mouth and looked in an oddly calm way at the blue vein standing out at his temple. "Get out of here," he said again.

"Oh, now, don't," said my aunt appeasingly, getting up.

I stood up. One of the tangerines fell and rolled across the floor.

"Kyoko dear, don't go. Make up with your father. Please." She held onto my arm, looking close to tears. "If you want to spend another year here studying, you're more than welcome to stay. I'd be delighted to have you. So please, both of you—"

"Let her go," my father growled, then got up and went into the next room.

I left the living room without another word. Back in my room, I put on a chocolate-brown jacket I was fond of, and wrapped a yellow scarf around my neck. I stuck my wallet, book of bus tickets and train pass in a pocket, and put on a pair of knitted gloves. As I was pulling on my boots by the front door, my aunt came running.

"Where are you going in all this snow? You haven't even had breakfast yet."

"Sorry," I said. "I just have to get away. You know what I mean?"

"But surely there's no need to walk out like this. Your father has to take the train back to Tokyo this afternoon. Make things right with him before he goes. He's worried sick about you. That's why he—"

I opened the front door and raised my umbrella against the thickly falling snow. The cold, wet smell of it was in the air.

"Kyoko!" said my aunt harshly.

I stepped out and closed the door behind me without looking back.

In the snow, it took the bus forever to come. I stood at the bus stop breathing on my hands to warm them, looking on idly as cars wearing tire chains made ruts in the snow, the sound curiously muffled and light. I got on the bus for Sendai Station, and by the time I got there it was nine o'clock. I wasn't hungry, but to warm myself up I went to a noodle stand and had a bowlful of hot soba noodles with an egg on top. I bought a pack of MF and some matches and went to the waiting room. There was a big oil stove there, and it was warm. An old woman returning from her rounds selling homegrown produce sat nodding off. I took a seat next to her and lit a cigarette.

My mind wouldn't function. My head felt empty, dizzy. I tried to think about Wataru, but I couldn't. I chain-smoked two cigarettes and felt my head swim, but I lit a third one anyway. The old woman next to me woke up, put a crumpled unfiltered cigarette in her mouth, and began patting her pockets in search of a match. I offered her one of mine and she thanked me.

I stayed in the waiting room 'til ten, then made my way to A Cappella, which had just opened. Inside, the strains of Bach's "Well-Tempered Clavier" filled the still-chilly air. Leaving my coat on, I sat in a front-row seat in the deserted room, ordered a coffee and closed my eyes.

Keep calm, I told myself. Mustn't get swept away by sentimentality or anger or anxiety. Put your emotions in boxes, arrange them and organize them, label them, stack them neatly in your head so that nothing spills out. Anything that does, you've got to have the courage to discard.

Mentally, I prepared several boxes. One for issues with my parents, one for the entrance exams, one for the future, one for Wataru… Taking an idealistic approach was wrong. I had to be intensely practical. One by one, I took up various problems and stuck them in a handy box. It felt like moving, when you don't know what to do with your junk and end up throwing anything and everything in with the household goods.

Filing things in mental boxes was unexpectedly easy. Maybe I had a greater ability to cope with reality than the next person. Once I made up my mind to do it, I could tackle my problems head-on, accept some sort of compromise, or leave them in the lurch. I suppose anyone could do as much if they really thought about their own best interests. What I lacked was the courage to control the welter of emotions that inevitably spilled out in the process.

I gave a sigh and sipped the cup of coffee a waiter brought me. My mind now contained stacks of neatly labeled boxes, but this solved nothing. A muddy stream of emotions spilled from them like raw sewage, overflowing in my head. I couldn't contain it. I thought of Wataru. The muddy water swirled and eddied around him. I no longer knew what I wanted from him or why he had such a hold over me.

I leaned my head against the wall and closed my eyes, at a complete loss. I felt drained and helpless. It was crazy. The words slipped out of my mouth: "This is crazy."

I sensed someone's presence nearby. I opened my eyes, and there in the narrow aisle stood Yunosuke, looking down at me. He was wearing a gray tweed coat and an olive brown scarf. He looked pretty damn sophisticated.

"What is?" he asked, a cigarette dangling from his lips.

"You heard that?" I laughed in embarrassment. "Nothing, just talking to myself."

"Playing hooky, are we?"

"It's a snow holiday," I said. "You college students are lucky. You get to cut class anytime you want."

"Not really." He gave a quick laugh and asked if he might join me.

I didn't ask why he was there alone, without either Wataru or Ema, and he didn't say. For a while we talked about generalities. That was when I felt most at ease with him. His way of relating to people, the space he maintained, was very similar to Wataru's, though he rarely retreated into a shell the way Wataru did, spurning intimacy with a fixed, artificial smile. He could be open and unrestrained – crude even, as when he engaged in heavy petting with Ema in front of Wataru and me – and yet sometimes he was like a small, highly strung animal, the sort that would bare its fangs and drive an intruder off, or die trying. That sort of animal.

Once the conversation reached a deeper level, he would get a nervous, sullen, almost belligerent look on his face. When he started in on a specific topic, no matter what it was – literature, music, anything at all – I felt as though I could see painfully raw nerves begin to protrude all over him. He was scathing if anyone trotted out a specious argument. He was borderline obsessive, I thought, but not really consistent – too cavalier for that.

Wataru understood him thoroughly and always steered clear of any tricky topic, but Ema would occasionally come out with some statement that raised his hackles. When this happened he ripped into her, leaving her in tears.

For all these reasons I often felt edgy around him, but looking back, I think Ema must have found his overbearing personality attractive. Again and again he reduced her to tears, and it only made her cling tighter than ever. I never heard her bad-mouth him behind his back or claim that he couldn't get along without her, like some housewife who thought she had the upper hand. She was gone on him. Madly, irrationally in love.

But my taste didn't run to neurotic, aggressive types. Yes, Yunosuke was alarmingly good-looking and could be smoothly charming, but for me he would always be impossible to relate to, too slippery to ever pin down.

This was the first time he and I had ever been alone together. I became self-conscious and felt myself tense up, which made me babble about nothing in particular. I told him about my quarrel with my father, making light of it. When I mentioned getting slapped the night before, he said with a chuckle, "Sounds like a good father to me."

"Why?"

"My dad's never slapped me, not once."

"Because he's decent, probably."

"Hah. He's gutless. Can't stand to have any trouble in the house. If he ever hit me, he knows I might lose it and do something he'd end up having to pay for. The thought of that's too much for him, that's all."

"He doesn't trust you."

"After high school, when I told him I wasn't going on to medical school, he didn't get mad, he just cold-shouldered me. From the next morning on, my little brother was his new pet. He's a first-year med student now. My dad's got no use for me whatever. When he sees me, all he does is make some half-assed compliment, stick to safe topics, and laugh mindlessly. I've never felt loved by my father. Not once."

"What about your mother? She must love you. You're the eldest."

He didn't answer this. Instead he asked, "You ever see your parents having sex?"

"No," I said, feeling uncomfortable.

"When I was in junior high, I used to watch mine every night. Night after night. They never missed unless one of them was sick. My room was just across from their bedroom. My brother's room was farther down the hall, so he never knew, but every night around eleven I'd hear the sound of their bedroom door being locked. *Click.* When I heard that, I'd tiptoe out and go stand in front of their door."

"But – how could you see anything if the door was locked?"

"It was an old-fashioned door, the kind with a big keyhole. If I put my eye to it, I could see inside. My parents' bed was along the opposite wall, and I had an unobstructed view."

I was silent. Yunosuke snorted with laughter and looked up at the ceiling. "They went at it hammer and tongs, never knowing I was watching. Out of consideration for my brother and me they never made a peep, but the bed made such a racket it didn't matter. After the first round, my dad would be lying on his back, panting, and she'd start to lick him down there. He'd whisper for her to knock it off, let him catch his breath, but she was relentless. My dad was always a pushover, so he'd try manfully to satisfy her. Sit up with a frazzled look on his face and give it another crack. She was a sex maniac. Never got enough. Sometimes on Sundays when I came back from somewhere I'd find her draped all over him on the living room sofa. The way she could wiggle her ass was downright slutty."

He swallowed. "What I don't understand is why a woman that horny never went after any other man. It was always him she was after, as if she wanted to suck up all his energy. Between his work as a doctor and the time he spent pleasuring her, he was worn out. He had no time left over to think about his kids or show them he cared. That's what I think. The poor bastard."

"Is your mother nice-looking?"

"Drop-dead gorgeous," he said. "That's according to my father. She's definitely on the good-looking side. More like a Western woman than a Japanese."

"Well, that must have been quite a turn-on, watching your gorgeous mother have sex." I meant it as a joke.

Yunosuke looked at me. A tremor crossed his handsome, impassive features. I backtracked quickly. "Or not. I really wouldn't know. I haven't ever seen my parents like that, after all."

"I never got excited watching them together. Not ever."

"Then why go on watching?"

"To remind myself that that's where I began, from that union. No, that's not entirely it. It was also to see my mother's raunchiness, for lack of a better word. I watched, thinking I never wanted anything to do with her again. I watched to make myself look straight at the dirtiest, raunchiest, most hideous sight in the world."

He only felt that way because his father loved his mother, not him, I thought, but I couldn't say so aloud. Yunosuke fidgeted, lit a cigarette, looked at me. The tremor was gone.

"You're lucky, Kyoko. You're a nice girl from a nice home."

"Not particularly, on either count."

"You come from a good family."

"No, my dad's just a boring company man."

"That's what 'good family' means. Come on, admit it."

I gave him a wordless smile to convey that I didn't agree, but it seemed not to register. He looked at his watch. "God, look at the time. I meant to stop in for a cup of coffee and get going right away. You were here, so I sat and yapped."

"Going home?"

"No, I'm off to the library. Gotta look something up. After that I'm seeing Ema."

"At your place?"

"No, Wataru needs to rest."

"Something wrong?"

"He said he felt a cold coming on. Nothing serious. Why don't you go pay him a call? He's probably bored silly."

Controlling the urge to jump up and rush out the door, I said thoughtfully, "Hmm. Yeah, I might do that."

Yunosuke nodded, got up and put on his coat. "Well, see you around."

"Hi to Ema."

"Yup."

No sooner was he out the door than a group of students came in. I took a slow drag on my cigarette, stubbed it out carefully in the ashtray, then requested Pachelbel's Canon.

When I closed my eyes, Wataru's face and Yunosuke's, too, rose in my mind, along with the unknown faces of Yunosuke's parents. Wataru and his sister making love in an old brass bed. Yunosuke spying on them through a keyhole, not in the least turned on by what he saw, his eyes dead. But peering through the keyhole on and on, watching them copulate.

When I called out at the crawl-in entrance to the teahouse, Wataru's voice greeted me: "That you, Kyoko? C'mon in."

I softly slid open the door, sat down, unlaced my boots and took them off. The wet laces were so cold that my fingertips went numb.

The snow was falling harder. Snow piled on bamboo leaves cascaded heavily to the ground. The stone lantern and the latticed bamboo gate were almost unrecognizable under their burden of snow.

"Heard you've got a cold. Are you okay?" I asked as I closed the door behind me. "I happened to run into Yunosuke at A Cappella, and he told me." I held out a bundle of tangerines, which he took with pleasure.

"I was just thinking how much I wanted to see you," he said, and looked straight at me. "You must be frozen. Your nose is bright red."

"Call me Rudolph."

He smiled and held up a corner of the old quilt they used as a *kotatsu* cover. "Get in and get warm."

On the tabletop was a lamp and a copy of Sei Ito's *Portrait of a Young Poet*. Wataru's face stood out in the pale lamplight. He didn't look well, but he had a slight growth of beard and looked more virile than usual. Awkwardly, I sat down and, to cover my embarrassment, felt his forehead with my hand.

"You've got a temperature."

"It's nothing."

"Shouldn't you be lying down?"

"I'm alright. Just enough fever to feel pleasantly light-headed."

I'd heard from my aunt that mushroom broth was good for a fever, or hot water poured over onion and pickled plum. I seriously considered making something for him, but in the end I didn't. It wasn't my style to fuss over someone like that, and anyway he clearly wasn't expecting it. So all I did was boil some water and make two cups of instant coffee.

This wasn't the first time we'd been alone together in the teahouse. The other times had always been brief. I'd go over and listen to records with Yunosuke and Wataru, and at some point Yunosuke would get up and disappear. I'd eye the entrance uneasily, wondering where he'd gone, until thirty or forty minutes later, an hour at most, he'd be back. That happened more than once.

Nothing would have made me happier than for Wataru to ask me over when his friend was out, but he never did. Even though they shared the place, Wataru was living there rent-free. I chose to believe that his failure to invite me there alone was a matter of simple etiquette.

But today was different. Yunosuke was at the library, and afterwards he had a date with Ema. He wouldn't be back 'til well after dark. Alone together for a whole day… my cold body warmed up and relaxed at the thought. I drank my coffee and talked at length about my quarrel with my father, about how he'd slapped me, about how I had no idea what tack he would take next. Unlike Yunosuke, Wataru never teased me about any of it.

"It's okay," he said. "College really isn't that big a deal. There's no law that you have to go, and even if you do, it doesn't change anything."

"Really? Nothing changed for you by going to college?"

"Not really."

"Why'd you go?"

"I didn't want to get a job. That's about it."

I nodded and told him I understood. "I've thought about it over and over 'til I'm sick of it. Why I want to go to college, I mean."

"What did you decide?"

I answered honestly. "So I can party, and drink, and feel really alive, and have people say, 'She may be a bitch but she's no dummy – look at the five-star school she got into.'"

He laughed and said, "You're too self-conscious."

I laughed too. "The upshot of it is, I think I'd better start hitting the books. After all, I do want to go to college."

"So you'll spend the coming year going to cram school?"

"Yes, but not in Tokyo," I said, warming my hands under the quilt. "I want to stay on here in Sendai. Nothing's going to change."

With a quick little intake of breath, he said, "Your dad'll let you?"

"I don't know. But I'll go through hell and high water to stay."

"Why is that?"

I looked up cautiously. One corner of his mouth was twisted.

"Why do you want to stay in Sendai so much?" he repeated. The question was not in the least ill-natured. He sounded completely innocent, the way a child sounds when it asks its parent something. I felt my throat constrict.

"Don't you know?" My voice shook a little. "Wataru, don't you know why I want to stay in Sendai?"

He was silent. To hide my shock, I lit a cigarette. "If you don't, that's all right," I said with a laugh, blowing out smoke. I racked my brains to come up with a lie. None came to mind.

"Won't you say it's because you don't want to leave me?" he asked quietly.

I looked at him. He smiled faintly and nodded. How could I say for certain that the smile was fake? I knew enough to suspect it might be insincere. But I tried hard to believe it. I wanted to.

"That's right," I murmured and closed my eyes. "It's because I don't want to leave you."

There was the sound of snow sliding off the roof. We both fell silent. More snow landed with a thud, rattling the teahouse window. After a long silence I opened my eyes. Wataru was looking at me.

What happened after that was perfectly ordinary. We did exactly the same thing that any boy and girl that age would have done. Even if it wasn't Wataru and me, it would have been no different. All the conditions were right: a small, cozy room shut off in a snowstorm. Close proximity. A roommate not due back 'til that night. A mixture of impatience and resignation over the future. A roundabout confession of love…

Wataru took my things off, not with the roughness he had displayed on my birthday, but with an almost otherworldly tenderness. They came off easily, so easily I was embarrassed.

I held perfectly still. His hot hand caressed my breast. He took his time, reassuring me and winning my trust before leaning me back onto the floor.

I closed my eyes and listened to the sounds of him undressing. First the sweater. Then the shirt buttons, then the shirt. The zipper was next. Then the jeans fell to the floor…

Slowly and deliberately, he laid himself on top of me. For a long time he caressed me. I was terribly nervous, my body stiff, but I did my best to enjoy it. Anything less would be impolite, I thought.

In the cold, unheated room, he was sweating. He was far more delicate in build than I'd imagined, his body like a flat-chested girl's. But there was a masculine strength to it. He was gentle yet commanding. He folded me tightly in his arms, and when I made the slightest move to close myself off to him, he prevented it with unexpected strength.

For a second his ragged breathing stopped. I felt fumbling movements down below. Oddly, I thought of Reiko. I could almost hear her whispering in my ear: "Get rid of it, honey." For the first time I realized I was exactly like every other girl in the world.

"Wataru," I whispered. "It's my first time. Please—"

He looked a little surprised, but quickly said, "I understand." He kept on stroking me, and slowly I felt myself soften. Everywhere he wasn't touching me was as cold as ice, but somewhere deep inside I felt a hot pulsing that spread slowly through my body, filling me like warm water, a brand-new, delicious sensation.

The rest I don't remember clearly. I know he put his fingers in my vagina and then tried to insert himself. It didn't work very well. He kept getting hard, then soft. When he got too soft he would rub himself vigorously. After several tries, finally he was inside me. I felt a twinge of pain, but it was bearable.

Still inside me, he whispered my name: "Kyoko… I love you." There was a trace of triumph in his voice. He seemed hugely powerful, hugely confident. He began to thrust his hips. Sharp pain like a menstrual cramp went through my abdomen. I said nothing, and the pain went away. In its place came something like a faint pleasure. It came in ripples, surging and receding and surging again.

Wataru gave a rough moan, went on whispering my name, then said something in the back of his throat that I couldn't catch, before collapsing limply on top of me. His sweat-soaked body lay over mine. My mind was numb and I couldn't speak. His body felt like a part of mine, but at the same time different, as if I'd been split in two.

He fondled my ear and covered me with moist kisses. Cautiously I opened my eyes. Overhead was the dark ceiling of the teahouse. The interior was bluish white, reflecting the snow outside. I couldn't think. For a while I just lay there and stared at the ceiling.

Through Wataru's heavy breathing, out of nowhere I thought I could hear a faint sound. I listened carefully. Amid a stillness so intense it hurt my ears, the sound slowly became distinguishable. In instinctive horror I raised my head.

The little door to the crawl space was halfway up, forming a perfect square. I could see fast-falling snow. Something appeared in the intermittent flurries – something like a dim vision of a freshly severed head. When I saw that it was Yunosuke's face, a shrill scream erupted from the back of my throat.

Wataru looked first at me, then following my line of sight, over to the door. Instantly the air froze and seemed to shatter into a million tiny, stabbing shards of ice.

Wataru was off me in a flash. "Fuck off," he hissed. "Get the hell out of here – now!"

Yunosuke sprang up. The hem of that familiar tweed coat swirled in the doorway. The door slammed shut, followed by the sound of footsteps running off haphazardly in the snow.

I curled into the fetal position and lay shivering, my arms crossed over my breasts. I couldn't believe what had just happened.

"He was watching," I said, my teeth chattering. "The whole time, for all we know…"

Wataru pulled me close. "Forget it. Please, forget about it."

"No!" I was crying like a baby. "What's wrong with him! Why would he *do* that? Why spy on us? Just when we were… like this…"

"It's okay now. It's okay." He held me, put his cheek next to mine, wiped away my tears with his fingers. My breath came in gulping sobs. I couldn't stop crying. I was remembering about the keyhole. Yunosuke was watching. He was always watching. Peering through a keyhole at people close to him as they had sex together.

"I don't… understand." The words came haltingly. "Is that… the kind of person he is?"

"No," said Wataru, burying his face in my hair. He let out a pained sigh. "No, it isn't."

That night I developed a fever. By the morning it was up to 102 degrees. My aunt was so worried that she sent for the doctor.

For three whole days I slept. I had a series of nightmares. Sometimes I dreamed of Yunosuke and Setsuko embracing; other times it was Wataru and Setsuko, or Wataru and Ema. Always the one spying through a keyhole was me. Though crazed with jealousy, I couldn't drag myself away. Then I saw Wataru and Yunosuke approach the keyhole, smirking. The keyhole grew dark, and I couldn't see anything. The next thing I knew, instead of me watching them, it was they who peered through it at me.

Usually I woke up screaming, but, even then, in my feverish state I would continue to hallucinate. I saw a girl in white come into my room through the door. She eased her way in and circled around my bed. She was featureless, cold, and sinister. I took a good look at her and saw a rope around her neck. It was the girl who'd hanged herself in my aunt's tool shed. I screamed again, but no sound emerged. *This is a dream*, I told myself. *Get a grip. Get rid of this creepy visitor. You're still alive, you're not dead.* I clenched my teeth and fought wildly. Gradually the paralysis of sleep gave way, and I could relax. The girl in white went out the door wearing a sorrowful expression. When I next woke up, for real this time, I was sopping wet with sweat.

On the fourth day, my fever finally went down and I was able to get out of bed. As I sat in the living room eating the rice porridge my aunt made for me, she said, "You've had several phone calls from a Mr. Domoto. Two or three a day. When I told him you were in bed with a fever, he sounded terribly worried."

"Oh," I said.

She smiled mischievously. "He's your boyfriend, isn't he, Kyoko?" When I didn't respond, she drew in her chin and held herself erect as she poured hot water in the teapot. "I can be understanding, you know."

I raised my face and looked at her.

She giggled and said cannily, "I *thought* something was going on between you two. He's called before this, too, hasn't he?" Then she relented. "All right. I won't tell your father, on one condition. I want you to stop this foolish quarreling with him."

"I promise," I said. "And I've decided that after graduation I'll go to a college prep school. I'm going to buckle down and study hard for a year. I really mean it this time."

"Well, the fever seems to have had a positive effect." She handed me a cup of green tea. "I'll be sure to tell your father."

"You don't have to," I said. "I'll tell him myself."

"Yes, that would be better," she agreed and then proceeded to question me about Wataru. I gave random answers until the questions grew more probing, at which point I excused myself, saying I was tired, and went back to bed.

I talked to Wataru on the phone that night. It was right after a joke-filled conversation with Juri, so I was able to sound fairly cheerful. We avoided discussing the events of four days ago and promised to get together soon, in a few more days. Just before hanging up, he said, "I love you." I nodded, feeling my eyes fill with tears, and gently laid the receiver in its cradle

8

In March I completed my application to a college prep school in Sendai, to start classes in April. My aunt enthusiastically urged my father to go along with this. I think she let slip something about what a comfort I was to her in her loneliness. In the end, as he cared a lot for his elder sister, he accepted her recommendation and allowed me to stay on there.

So in my final year of high school I never did take any college entrance exams. As a last gesture of defiance, on graduation day Juri, Reiko, and I stood by the school's main gate and passed out flyers we'd printed ourselves that said, "To Hell with Graduation!" For a while the scene was a madhouse as teachers flocked around trying to get us to stop, underclassmen cheered us on at a distance, other seniors heckled us loudly, and parents looked on in frowning concern.

Satisfied, we declined to attend the ceremony and made our exit. A lesbianish second-year student, a fan of Juri's, came running after us to the bus stop and handed her a rose corsage before running away again, crimson-faced. We howled with laughter as we got on the bus to our usual ramen place on Aoba Street, where we had some miso ramen before wandering around.

Juri, who loathed any sentimental display or formality, went on behaving as if it was a perfectly ordinary day, and Reiko and I followed suit. When we finally parted, we waved goodbye and said only "See you." Nobody added "Take care" or "It's been fun" or anything like that.

One week later, Juri went to stay with a friend in Tokyo. Reiko and I saw her off at Sendai Station, but again all we did was goof around and never said any formal goodbyes.

After she was gone, Reiko and I went to A Cappella for a coffee, had a rambling conversation about nothing much, and left. On parting, Reiko said in that sweet, languid way of hers, "Fare thee well."

"You know," I told her, "I've always loved the way you say that. Keep on saying it for me, will you?"

"I'll say it all you like," she replied. "Can we meet again?"

"Of course. I'm going to be here another year, don't forget."

"Want to know something? I'm feeling kind of lonesome. Juri's gone, and now you're going to be studying for exams night and day. I feel bereft."

"It suits you, though, Reiko. I'd never believe it anyway if you said something trite about staying positive."

"You're a good person." She blinked her big, sleepy-looking eyes. "I'll call you."

I promised I'd call her too.

That was the last time I ever saw her. That summer she took off to get married, and she and her husband, a doctor, went to live in Germany. I never found out what he was like. I heard only that he was ten years older and a graduate of the Tohoku University School of Medicine; a balding, short, fat guy whom she rather outclassed.

Later on I found out there was a bit more to it than that. The day we saw Juri off at the station and parted in front of A Cappella, Reiko took the train north to Yamagata, went into the snow-covered mountains and tried to kill herself. She survived because she didn't take a fatal overdose and because the owner of the inn where she was staying noticed she'd been acting strangely and called the police, so a search party went out that night.

The incident was briefly reported in the local paper, but the article didn't come to the attention of any of her acquaintances back home. After twice surviving suicide attempts, she apparently decided for reasons of her own, without telling anyone, to marry the doctor, who had always been keen on her.

It was so like her. She had actually tried to carry out that "new way to die" she'd dreamed up, of going up into the mountains and "chewing Hyminal or Brovarin or something till it turns sweet in your mouth." But then when things didn't go according to plan, she'd been forced to extensively rewrite the scenario. When the man she'd most wanted to care about her – the one who was supposed to bear the cross of her suicide for as long as he lived – didn't react the way she'd hoped, she threw in her lot with the other candidate, the balding, short, fat doctor. This, at least, is what I imagine happened. She was the sort of person who couldn't live without any man at all.

In the end, I don't know whether there was a bond between us or not. Just when I needed her most, ready to tell her everything and ask her advice, she vanished. I was never capable of opening up my heart to my friends, and neither, apparently, was she. She walked away from me without ever breathing a word of whatever secret it was that made her try to end her life.

Our personalities were like positive and negative versions of each other. She knew nothing of the outer surface of the world but was thoroughly acquainted with its underside, while I was the exact opposite. I understood the fringes of life and managed to find my way in them one way or other, but about life's messy interior I was pathetically ignorant.

There must have been countless times when Reiko and I needed each other, but opportunities always seemed to slip by. That didn't put a damper on our friendship, though. I liked her. Even now, twenty years since I last saw her, I remember her vividly and with real fondness.

Once I started at the prep school, when I wasn't with Wataru I was mostly studying. It wasn't at all unpleasant to take my seat amid the crowded rows of hard plain wooden chairs and plug away alongside the others. I was just one among many, and if I skipped class or came late or daydreamed, nobody cared. There was no one to fight with, no one to sympathize with, no one to say things that gave me food for thought. I always went alone to class, and afterwards I would sit in the empty room and study, heading out at suppertime to a neighborhood bistro for a plate of spaghetti that was garishly red with ketchup before going back to my books.

There were a few people there whom I knew slightly. One had been injured in an anti-war demonstration and came to class wrapped in bandages, hobbling on crutches. Another broke four front teeth in the struggle against the opening of the new airport; he grinned at me with a swollen purple mouth. He and the others would come up and say things like, "Hey there, Noma. Birds of a feather!" I ignored them all.

Once in a while – once in a very rare while – on my way home I would stop off at the park and join in a folk song rally. Sometimes the sight of a line of demonstrators gave me such a frisson of excitement that I wanted to throw everything to the winds and jump in. But instead I would return to my desk to memorize English idioms and the names of historical eras. My goal was horribly clear.

My determination not to be distracted left me more and more isolated from the times I lived in, I suppose; but if it did, what did it matter? No one spends every waking moment thinking about the world around them. Sometimes a person can drown in the everyday. It amused me to think of myself as a drowned body floating on the waves of the times. Being drowned was fine with me. It definitely had its perks. The waves were rough and sometimes cold, but a dead body remained insensible. All I'd have to do was wait to wash up purple and bloated on a beach somewhere.

Weekdays were mostly spent going from my aunt's house to school and back. It seems to me that Wataru and I saw each other almost daily, but I'm not sure how we managed to find the time. We must have stayed in constant communication, and met after class in the park or a coffee shop for a short while.

After what had happened with Yunosuke, I stopped going to the teahouse in Kitayama as much, but, even so, I would show up a couple of times a month, on Sundays. Ema was usually there too, and Wataru and I were never on our own. When we wanted to be alone, we would go to a by-the-hour hotel that was clean and cozy and quiet. For a good two hours we would kid around, and touch each other, and make love.

I was happy. It was as fleeting as a burst of fireworks, but after I fell in love with him, I was never so happy as then. It seemed that he had distanced himself from both Setsuko and Yunosuke, and set his sights exclusively on me.

Between slightly damp sheets, Wataru would ask me all sorts of questions. Starting with my early childhood, my elementary school years, my parents and my sister, he asked steadily more probing questions about every aspect of my history. Without noticing how much time had passed, I answered everything. I enjoyed being interrogated. The substance of the questions didn't matter. Just the thought that his eyes were turned on me was enough to make me shiver with happiness.

What did Wataru really feel as he embraced me, plied me with questions and carried on like this in the hotel? I often wondered later. He seemed so utterly natural, so full of passion! How could I have imagined that after scooping me into his arms, finding out all he could about me, kissing me and smiling happily all the while, he might have bouts of solitary anguish – that he might lie on his back and stare at the ceiling, biting his lips hard enough to draw blood? It was impossible to imagine this kind of thing.

Did I miss the signs because I was an inexperienced girl of eighteen? I don't think so. Not even a woman who'd slept with a thousand men, had a thousand affairs, would ever have thought he was putting on a show.

Every so often I would say something critical about Yunosuke. I said straight out that he was obsessive and perverted, a plain old nasty peeping Tom. I said he couldn't be trusted. I even said that for the life of me I couldn't understand how Wataru could be friends with him.

Wataru listened sympathetically. Sometimes he brought up episodes that backed up what I was saying, or admitted that Yunosuke wasn't a comfortable friend to be around. I would have to say now that this was an act, but at the time, hearing him chime in with my criticisms convinced me that, deep down, he disliked Yunosuke. The thought pleased me and fed my malice, and my criticisms became more scathing over time.

On the surface, Yunosuke treated me no differently than before. Seeing no change in his manner, sometimes I wondered if I had imagined that snowy day. He spoke in the same indifferent, worldly-wise way as ever, unconcerned with Ema's innocent affections. It was impossible to tell what he was thinking. He'd be silent and distant, then abruptly tell a zany joke and roar with laughter.

I often came close to asking him why he'd spied on us that day, but I never quite knew how to bring it up. The episode had settled like thick sediment in my mind, an unpleasant, disturbing incident that would never go away; yet it seemed pointless to turn to the person responsible for it all for help in getting over it.

I tried to believe that Yunosuke had nothing to do with Wataru and me. It was Wataru I loved, not him. Just because they remained roommates, there was no reason to get unduly upset that he'd seen us being intimate. If he intruded any further on our relationship, we could always take steps to see that it didn't happen again. There was any number of ways to do that.

It wasn't Yunosuke who struck me as strange so much as Ema. After graduating from high school, she had proceeded smoothly to the college attached to her school, but at some point I realized that she no longer looked anything like a typical college coed. Part of it was the heavier makeup she took to wearing, and the greater sophistication of the clothes, she bought with money wheedled out of her father. But that wasn't all. I can't quite explain it; it was almost as if she'd skipped the chrysalis stage and gone straight to being a butterfly. She had a sudden new sexiness about her. Though possibly unaware of it herself, overnight she'd taken on a disconcertingly adult appearance. Sometimes it was hard to believe that she and I could be the same age.

I think she was doing her utmost to rise to Yunosuke's level. When she opened her mouth to say something, she sounded as girlish as ever, but when silent she seemed to be wafting about on a higher plane somewhere.

She hung around Yunosuke most days. She'd have lunch or dinner with him, and if neither were possible she'd go to his place in the evening, knowing Wataru would be there, and quietly try to chase Wataru away. She couldn't let a day go by without seeing Yunosuke. It wasn't that she was trying to monopolize him; she loved him to the point of addiction.

Once she confessed to me how she felt: "Days I don't see him are hell. I can't do or think about anything else. As long as I can see him, I'm happy, even if it's just for a little bit. It's weird, I know. Go ahead, call me crazy. Even if he gets mad at me or treats me like I'm underfoot, I still want to be with him. Have you any idea what that's like? I've got no pride at all. Zilch. Even if he told me, 'I don't like you anymore, Ema. You're a drag. Let's split up,' you know what I'd say? One word: 'No.' That's all. A girl with a smidgen of pride wouldn't take it lying down if the boy she liked talked to her that way. She'd say, 'Okay, fine,' or else maybe sob and bring up old grudges. But not me. I'm done with self-respect. Whatever he said to me, I'd go crawling back just the same. It wouldn't make any difference."

"What if he ran off and you didn't know where to find him?" I asked.

She laughed. "I'd fix it so that he couldn't. I know a trick or two. When you haven't got any pride, you can do anything."

"But how? You're weaker than he is; you can't just pin him down and hogtie him."

"Oh, there are ways. Like stripping him bare while he's sleeping, then taking all his clothes and underwear and shoes and hiding them somewhere so he can't go out…"

I nodded, impressed. Ema, I could see, was confident in her belief that love would work out even when two people's feelings weren't on the same track. Her logic was screwy, and I certainly wasn't buying it, yet I could understand how she felt. I was jealous of the way she could boldly push forward, paying no attention to the shredded emotions she left behind.

That year, with both of us out of high school, Ema and I grew closer. As she lived only to see Yunosuke, and I was busy studying for exams, thinking only of seeing Wataru, we rarely made time for long, private get-togethers; even so, before long she was calling me up at my aunt's house about once a week.

Once Ema got started talking, she wouldn't hang up. It was all silly, innocent girl talk; the same sort of endless, joking conversations I used to have with Juri and Reiko. It seemed both as if she was chattering away because she didn't want to hang up, and as though she felt free to rattle on about anything she liked just because it was me on the other end of the line.

My aunt frowned disapprovingly more than once. Out of consideration for her, I would try to cut the conversation short. "Oops, sorry," Ema would say, and back off. "Sorry I bothered you. Talk to you later. See you at the teahouse."

Time and again, I thought of telling her about how Yunosuke had watched Wataru and me the first time we had sex. Of course, so she wouldn't misunderstand, I planned to add that it was all a coincidence. There was no reason not to tell her. She wasn't the type to go into shock, or make a big deal out of it and confront Yunosuke, demanding an explanation. She would probably find it an amusing anecdote, nothing more, and soon forget about it. His existence itself was the sole focus of her attention; what he may have seen or felt wouldn't be of any great concern.

There were so many things I wanted to tell her about Wataru, and me, and the strange intimacy between Wataru and his sister… If, on the night of a late-August typhoon, I hadn't gone to Kitayama and seen what I did, I might have told her everything. I was really starting to like her.

There'd been no word from Juri, off in Tokyo. Not knowing that Reiko had attempted suicide and then plunged into marriage, I telephoned her house, only to be told several times that she had "gone to the countryside." I felt a vague sense of betrayal. I was starving for someone to confide in. Since Ema knew both Wataru and his sister, as well as the ins and outs of his friendship with Yunosuke, she was the logical choice. In fact, she would have been perfect.

But before I could divulge any of my harmless secrets, what happened, happened. I became confused; I went nearly wild with distraction. Ema was the last thing on my mind. Thoughts of every friend I'd ever had were far away. I was isolated, and in my isolation I racked my brains about what to do. I didn't give Ema a thought until long afterwards. I wish to God I'd thought about her sooner. I wish to God I'd opened up to her right away. I should have. Even today, twenty years later, the regret and the guilt are keen.

That day, the last Saturday in August, the weather was bad due to an approaching typhoon. My aunt had plans to meet an old school friend up at Lake Towada and spend the night at an inn there, but that morning the unpromising weather made her reconsider.

"By tonight all of Tohoku will be caught up in the storm," she said. "Maybe it would be better to put the trip off."

"Look," I said, "you're not going there for a swim in the lake. You went to all the trouble of getting a reservation, so why not go ahead and go? You haven't seen your friend in a long time, right?"

I was determined to pack her off as scheduled. Having known for some time that she'd be away, I was counting on having Wataru stay the night. He knew all about it of course, and was scheduled to drop by later in the evening. I didn't care a fig about the typhoon; nothing, but nothing, was going to wreck my well-laid plans.

"True," she sighed, flipping channels to check the unchanging weather forecast for the umpteenth time. "But there's no reason why I have to go today of all days. We could talk over old times right here in town, as far as that goes. That's a thought. Why not just invite her down to Sendai?"

"You're going to ask someone who lives way up north to come all the way here?" I said. "That's a bit much. If anything, *you* should offer to go there."

"True," she said again. In the end, apparently the prospect of cancelling her reservation, contacting her friend and changing all their arrangements was just too much trouble. With several apprehensive glances at the blustery sky, she summoned a taxi and left.

I stayed at home that day and spent the afternoon holed up in my room, studying. At dusk I went out to the neighborhood supermarket to pick up some ingredients for supper. By the time I set to work in the kitchen, wild gusts of wind and rain were rattling the windowpanes with an eerie sound. Even then I didn't give the typhoon much thought at all. I set the living room table with a lace tablecloth and put fresh covers on the cushions. I made my bed, cleaned the toilet, put out a fresh bar of soap.

When I had finished making some beef curry – the one dish I prided myself on – I went out to meet Wataru, stepping out with Mogu into the rain-swept lane. There was always the chance that neighbors would later tell my aunt that I'd taken advantage of her absence to sneak a boy into the house, but that day everyone's shutters were fastened and all was quiet.

I went up and down the lane twice, then out to the bus stop. There was no sign of him. I went back inside, tied Mogu up in the shed and fed him before going to my room. It was already seven o'clock. A strange gloom had settled in with the typhoon.

He was supposed to come at six thirty, but seven thirty passed and still he didn't appear. At exactly eight o'clock the telephone rang in the living room. I sprang to the receiver, but it wasn't Wataru's voice I heard; it was my aunt's. She was concerned about my safety and full of advice – I should light a candle right away if the electricity went out, I should run to a neighbor's house if I got scared – but I scarcely listened.

At eight forty-five there was a news alert: a severe storm warning had been issued for Miyagi prefecture. The rain fell harder and harder. With the shutters closed, the room was sticky and humid, and the freshly changed cover on my cushion was already damp. I paced around the house, listened to the wind and rain at the front door, then returned to the living room and stared at the clock on the wall.

Nine o'clock went by, and nine fifteen. Something sudden must have come up, I told myself. At the same time I knew that whatever it was, he could have phoned – unless he'd been in an accident. The thought went round and round in my head, making it impossible to sit still. I imagined him lying crushed under a giant sign ripped loose in the wind, or hit by a car that had skidded in the rain-slick street. At nine thirty I made up my mind, grabbed my wallet, and flew outside.

If only there'd been a phone line to the teahouse. That thought would torment me for years to come. If it had been equipped with a telephone, I could have called Wataru, found out that something had indeed come up, and stuffed myself with cold beef curry in disappointment. There'd have been no need to go all the way over to his place. I could have spent the rest of the night imagining what might have been and filling the peach can with cigarette butts. And that would have been that.

But there's no point wishing now that Yunosuke had had a telephone. Back then, the vast majority of students living alone had no direct access to anything as convenient as that. In case of an emergency, often the landlord would pass on a message. Some apartment buildings may have had a public telephone in the hallway, but in Sendai this was rare. Besides, Yunosuke was staying in a detached teahouse, and had nothing to do with his landlord or his family. The thought of calling the landlord and asking him to summon Wataru to the phone was simply out of the question; it never once occurred to me.

Outside the typhoon may have been in full swing, but I have no memory of how violent it was. My mind was focused entirely on

the possibility that Wataru had been in an accident and carted off
to a hospital. If I went to the teahouse across town, I might learn
something. I could at least ask Yunosuke what he knew. Clinging
to that hope, I went out into the street and walked around for some
time in the driving rain, hunting for a taxi. By the time I finally
flagged one down and made it across town, it was probably close to
ten thirty. I stopped the taxi in front of Ando Dental Clinic, paid the
fare, and slipped through the hole in the hedge.

The garden behind the main house was pitch dark, cut off from
the light of the streetlamps, and buffeted by wind and rain. The trees
made an eerie whistling sound. Thunder rumbled in the distance,
and an occasional flash of lightning lit up the darkness with a burst of
bluish-white light. Gripping my half-closed umbrella, I scampered
over the slippery, glistening black stepping-stones.

Faint light filtered from the main house behind me through the
wildly thrashing branches, flickering like a will-o'-the-wisp. The
loud rustle of bamboo sounded in my ears. Thunderclaps alternated
with lightning flashes at ever-shorter intervals. The rain slanted
sideways, making my umbrella virtually useless. Drenched from the
shoulders down, I came to a stop just in front of the teahouse.

The lights weren't on. The small window gave off a dim glow. In
the faint light I could make out a large, swaying silhouette. It looked
something like the movements of a bug inside a lantern, cast on the
wall as a shadow picture.

I felt nothing then. If someone had lit a candle, what was strange
about that? I assumed that the teahouse's power had gone out. Of
greater concern was the evidence that someone was at home. What
if it was Yunosuke and Ema, and Wataru wasn't there? What would
I do then? That new thought filled my mind.

The idea of barging in on them as they sat snuggled together in
candlelight on the night of a typhoon, with me wailing that I didn't
know where Wataru was or why he'd broken his date with me – that
I was worried he'd had some dreadful accident – made me lose my
nerve. Even supposing they had no idea where he was, they couldn't
very well let me turn around and head back into the teeth of the
storm. Naturally they would insist that I come in and sit awhile, but
the last thing I wanted to do was intrude on Ema's turf. Besides, I

was worried to death about Wataru, in no mood to sit and make small talk while affecting a calmness I didn't feel.

Abruptly a horrible suspicion crossed my mind. What if Wataru had another girlfriend? Someone far more grown-up and attractive than little Kyoko Noma. Someone only Yunosuke knew about. What if Yunosuke knew all along that Wataru was going to break his date with me in order to see her tonight?

Strangely, I'd never suspected Wataru of cheating on me before. Apart from Setsuko, I'd never imagined him caring about any other girl. I gulped; it sounded quite loud in my ears. Doubts that my suspicion could be true mingled with the knowledge that if it were true, I was a hopeless idiot. A second's calm reflection might have reassured me, but I stood petrified in the storm, not knowing what to do.

My umbrella was in danger of blowing away, so I closed it, exposing myself to the full force of the rain and wind as I crept closer. A piercing thunderclap sent a tremor through the ground underfoot, but it didn't scare me. I was determined to see Yunosuke. See him and find out where Wataru was, learn from him what had gone wrong tonight. I remembered something Ema had once said: *I'm done with self-respect.* She was right. Swallow your pride, and there's no stopping you.

The wind whipped my wet hair and plastered it against my cheeks. I went up to the crawl-in entrance. The door was half open, and from inside came the glow of candlelight. There was a flash of lightning, then a peal of thunder that roared through the earth. This time I cowered in fright, but I didn't freeze. Standing under the eaves, I reached for the door.

Two pale, naked bodies were locked together in a circle of light. I can't claim that I didn't understand what it meant, but I had never seen such a thing before, nor really heard about it, either. I can't remember ever discussing it with anyone. But I was aware that such forms of love did exist.

I lost my voice and the power of thought. I didn't collapse in shock or start to cry. I simply could not move.

The candlelight wavered and Wataru, grasped firmly from behind by Yunosuke, turned his face slowly towards the open door. He was sweaty, the look on his face a mix of rapture and agony. His eyes were open but he gave no sign of seeing me.

Amid the rain, the wind and the thunder, their groans and the sound of flesh on flesh were equally inaudible to me. Wataru's eyes swam, then he reached behind and grabbed Yunosuke's sturdy arm. At this gesture they came apart, and slowly turning face to face, wrapped their arms fiercely around each other. Yunosuke now had his back to me and Wataru's face was turned in my direction, over Yunosuke's shoulder.

There was another flash of lightning. The room turned blue like the bottom of a swimming pool. Wataru's gaze hung in space, completed an arc, and came to rest on me.

It happened in a split second. I saw him flinch. He may have shouted out. He may have called my name. Or maybe it was Yunosuke's name that he called out. In any case, I didn't catch what he said. Before I knew it, I was running in tears through the storm-tossed garden.

9

There were no more buses at that hour, and I didn't have the patience to wait for a taxi. Instead I ran through the rain. I ran 'til it hurt, then stopped to catch my breath before running again. At long last, I was standing at the narrow lane that led to my aunt's house.

The moment I stepped inside the front door I recovered my wits. The wind had wrecked the spokes on my umbrella, and I was as wet from head to toe as if I'd jumped into the sea fully clothed. I crouched down on all fours. Sobs shook my chest and throat. I wept in convulsive spasms that swept through me like waves of nausea. I cried and cried and cried.

When no tears were left, I went to the bathroom and took my wet things off. I had no energy to run a fresh bath, so I just sat down, ran some cold water in the basin and splashed it over my head. I didn't know what I was doing or what I would do next. I just wanted to be doing something. Needing to punish myself, to hurt myself physically somehow, I threw buckets of cold water on myself. My hair streaming, I cried some more.

At some point I got up and wrapped myself snugly in a dry towel, and smoked three cigarettes in a row. The wind and rain were stronger than ever. The house shivered and rattled, but my mind was eerily calm and blank. If one's mind is ever really incapable of thought, it is at times like this. Sobs rose uncontrollably and tears streamed down my face, but I felt strangely detached, on a plane far removed from shock, despair, emptiness, or any other expected state of mind. I had even forgotten what it was that had put me in this daze in the first place.

My wet body still wrapped in the towel, I went to my stifling room and crawled into bed. I took deep breaths and pressed my face into the pillow, but it was no use: I felt no sense of reality. The dryness of the sheets against my skin, the smell of sunlight from my pillow, even the occasional moans that escaped my mouth – all seemed unreal, as if this were only some movie I was watching.

I was afraid of the pain becoming real. I wanted to remain forever in this limbo. To avoid looking reality in the face I lay in bed for ages, sprawled under the covers like a drunk.

How much time went by? After a while, out in the yard Mogu gave a low growl. Perhaps because of the wind, it sounded startlingly close. He growled menacingly and began to howl.

The front doorbell rang, and I jerked up in bed. Reality came flooding back. For a moment I couldn't move, as if trapped in an air pocket between the end of one nightmare and the beginning of another.

The doorbell rang twice more, stopped for a while, rang again. Mogu was howling frantically now. That's when I realized I was naked. I threw the bath towel on the floor and went over to my chest of drawers, grabbed some underwear and put it on, then pulled a floral print dress on over my head. As I was struggling with the back zipper, someone started to knock on the front door. I knew perfectly well who it was.

The zipper stuck. I bit my lip – bit it so hard that I tasted blood. Then all at once, like a dam bursting, the sadness I had staved off came rushing in. Again I saw Wataru and Yunosuke in each other's arms, the scene recurring with such vividness that I could have sworn they were there before my eyes. My hands still gripping the back of my dress, I sank heavily to the floor.

The word "homosexual" never crossed my mind. Knowledge of the deep intimacy the two men shared brought only a spate of violent emotions: jealousy, regret, hate. From the start it had been impossible to wedge myself between them. Wataru and I would never be a couple now. And yet I'd loved him, wanted him. I'd accepted Yunosuke as his best friend. Whatever illusions I may have been under, I'd been sure that Wataru and I were a couple in love.

There was pounding on the door, followed by the doorbell, then more pounding. Intermittently, Mogu's howls and the fury of the wind blocked out all other sounds.

"Kyoko!" Wataru's voice came from beyond the door. It was surprisingly loud. "Open up, will you? Come on!"

I was scared to open the door. Why had he walked all the way here in this storm? Maybe what I thought I'd witnessed was somehow a mistaken impression on my part, something to laugh about when I heard the truth. Wataru, having realized this, had come to set the record straight. Wasn't that it? I tried to think so, but it was no use. How could there be any mistake? What was I supposed to think, that they'd been horsing around? That they'd been drinking and were just having a little romp? No. I'd seen what I'd seen.

Wataru kept knocking. I got up, went out of the room and stood by the front door. From a house nearby came the sound of shutters sliding open. Mogu's noisy, insistent barking had started to attract attention. Deciding I couldn't ignore it any longer, I worked up the nerve to unlock the door.

Wataru stood there, his white shirt sopping wet. His hair, battered by the wind and rain, hung down over his bloodshot eyes like strands of withered vines. Shock had distorted my sense of perspective; he seemed to stand far away. It was as if the doorway itself was distant, and beyond it stood someone pocket-sized.

He looked at me and said, "Sorry to come so late." His voice was a feeble rasp. "I need to talk to you. Now. It can't wait."

His voice sounded remote. My ears rang, and his words resonated dully somewhere inside my head. I felt a spell of faintness coming on. I took a deep breath and pressed a hand to my forehead. My legs wobbled. I felt sick. Wataru slipped inside the door and held my arm in support. I brushed him off.

He looked down at me, frowning, his jaw clenched. A trickle of rain ran down his temple.

"Now listen to me," he said. "You've got to listen."

Don't fall to pieces, I told myself. If I went to pieces now, I would only make a fool of myself. This wasn't disappointed love; it was something unimaginably worse.

I thought of the Simon and Garfunkel song, "I Am a Rock." That would be me. I would make myself hard as a rock, shut myself off. Whatever I heard now, I wouldn't flinch. Whatever happened, I wouldn't waver. Cold as stone. Whether I could manage it I had no idea, but the main thing, I felt, was to say nothing. Once I started talking, that would be it: a torrent of ugly words would burst out, swallowing any sense in me and leaving me without a shred of dignity.

I got up without a word, fetched a white towel from the washroom, and handed it to him. I can't recall whether he had an umbrella or not. In any case, he was wet to the skin. He took the towel, but didn't wipe himself dry. "I'm coming in," he said. I nodded and made way.

He went into my room. I didn't care about the messed-up bed, the bath towel on the floor, the open drawers. I stood motionless in the middle of it, forgetting even that the zipper on my dress was half undone.

He looked at me, arms dangling in apparent exhaustion. The silence grew oppressive. *This is all a joke*, I thought. A really bad joke. A howler. Maybe we'd burst out laughing, fall into each other's arms and kiss, then roll around on the bed as usual.

But Wataru didn't laugh. Neither did he grin at me comically and say, "Now, I hope you didn't get the wrong idea." He merely glanced at me, his shoulders heaving with each breath, his face pitifully twisted in a look of pain, as if at any moment tears might come.

"I never thought I'd have to talk about this," he said. "Especially not to you, of all people…"

I said nothing. He fixed me with a look, then raised both arms and tore at his hair. The gesture did not seem theatrical. Clearly he felt frantic and at a loss.

I guessed that he was about to launch into a long story… a long and harrowing story. Why is it that people can't help listening to the things they least want to hear? Knowing that once they hear it nothing will ever be the same, that they'll never recover, why do they still want to know?

I wanted to know, and I didn't. I had the sensation of standing in front of a fortune-teller famous for predicting how one would meet one's end. Part of me wanted to take to my heels, but another part felt that no matter what he said, it was far better to know the truth.

Wataru told me to sit down somewhere, and he seated himself on my bed, still dripping wet. I sat on the floor and leaned against the stereo. The half-open zipper at my back felt chilly, pressing hard into my sweaty skin.

He was silent for a long time. The silence dragged on so long that I thought perhaps he had gone to sleep. Unable to bear it any longer, I raised my face, just as he opened his mouth to speak.

"You may find this unbelievable," he said.

Out of the corner of my eye I saw him perched on the edge of the bed, his face a vague dark shadow. I kept my eyes straight ahead, focusing on a blot of ink on the wallpaper.

"I… loved Yunosuke. And he loved me. We were…"

Slowly I closed my eyes, and rolled them heavenward. Still with no sense of reality, my mind focused desperately on one question: how to deal with this absurd confession. No solution presented itself.

"I don't know how to explain it. I really can't explain how we got this way, but we did. However hard I tried to pull myself away from him, I couldn't do it… and neither could he."

From my closed eyes, something hot overflowed and ran down my cheeks.

"Don't cry, Kyoko," he said. "If you cry, I won't be able to speak."

I opened my eyes and shook my head, sniffling. "I don't get it," I said. "I just don't get it. You never cared about me from the beginning. So why—"

The sound of the storm beating against the windowpanes let up a little, and in the momentary silence I heard the bed give an awkward squeak beneath him.

"I do care about you. I do, Kyoko. I fell in love with you, and that hasn't changed."

"I don't get it," I repeated. I said it over and over. I felt like saying it forever. The back of my nose grew hot, my throat trembled, I felt dizzy. "What does loving another man mean? If you love him, how could you love me?"

"I don't have an answer for that. I wish I did. But it's hard. I don't even know how to explain it. I'm confused too; I've been confused a long time, ever since I met you. But one thing is certain. I care about you. I can't help it, I just do. I've been trying to distance myself from Yunosuke. Really. I thought it would never happen again. Because no matter how much I loved him, I couldn't love both of you at once. So—"

"I made beef curry for you," I whimpered. "I was waiting for you to come. I cleaned the toilet and I put out a nice tablecloth. It was going to be our first night together. That was all I could think about. When I realized you weren't coming I got frantic, afraid something had happened to you. I thought Yunosuke would know. That's why I went there. There was a candle lit inside, so I thought the power must have gone off. I didn't mean to pry. I was just going to pop in for a second. I thought it was him and Ema. I was sure of it. And then – I saw inside."

I blubbered like a child. My face, I knew, was ugly and twisted from crying, but I didn't care. Sobbing, I went on. "Yunosuke wasn't… with Ema. He was… with you."

The sight of Wataru on all fours came back to me. He'd been moaning, his eyes swimming in space – full of pain and ecstasy.

My knowledge of sex was mostly vicarious and I had no real understanding of "perverted" sex, but I remembered an English word I'd heard in a movie somewhere: *sodomy*. I didn't know how to say it in Japanese, but I knew what it meant. I knew all too well.

"You're going to hate me now," said Wataru in a low voice. "I know that. But I still want you to know why I stood you up tonight. That's why I came. You may think I'm just making excuses for myself, and you may despise me more than ever. Either way, it's all right. I have to tell you. I want you to listen. No matter what you think of me, you're the one person I have to tell."

I blew my nose and looked at him. His lips were dry and pale, almost bloodless. He nodded to himself slightly, then slowly closed his eyes. The lamp on my desk made deep shadows on his face. His face – the look on his face – was consummately beautiful. I have never seen another man with quite that look; beyond masculinity or virility or sex appeal, it had a pure, classic beauty. He was like a work of art – a figure lost in thought, or a portrait whose expression changes with the light.

I felt a surge of blind hatred for Yunosuke. Incredibly, he had become my rival in love. Whether he was male or female didn't matter. He was the one who made my relationship with this strikingly beautiful man a love triangle. I was fighting him over Wataru, and tonight he had won. Wataru had broken his date with me for an evening of hard sex with Yunosuke. Tonight I was the clear loser.

"Yunosuke was always jealous of you."

I looked up. Wataru shrugged a little, twisted his mouth, and said, "Yeah, he was. Funny, isn't it?" He tried to laugh, but it didn't come off. Silently I turned my eyes away.

"For a long time – a good two years – we hadn't been... together that way. We'd promised each other to quit. Both of us are capable of loving women, so we figured that's what we'd better do. The decision came naturally. Life's easier that way. While everybody else in this generation, you included, was off protesting the war and calling for peace, rioting on campus, marching in demonstrations, throwing rocks at riot police and so on, the two of us were in our own little world. If we were more like you, we might have stood up for the legitimacy of that world. As you probably know, there are plenty of precedents. It's not only us by a long shot. There was no need for us to stay holed up in that little room like a pair of sexual outcasts. But... we never thought of claiming a right to go on the way we were. Not in the least. We couldn't look at it that way. Didn't see any need. We wanted to go on turning our backs on convention, the way we were. Living 'in sin.' We were like a couple of insects hiding out in a dark, damp place. You know the creepy-crawlies you find out in a cranny somewhere, under a rock? The kind that when you pick up the rock, they're so blinded by the sun that they curl up in a ball and burrow into the ground? That was us. We didn't have the assurance or the strength to go on that way our whole lives, but that's how it was. It had to end. We talked about it again and again, and we both agreed. We felt exactly the same way. We knew we were capable of loving women. That's the truth. We didn't know how deeply we could love a woman, but there was no reason not to try. Because after all... neither of us was born to love another man."

He bit his lip. I saw the pale lip turn faintly red, then lose color again.

"When Ema came along we both felt saved. You know what a great kid she is, and how sexy. Yunosuke was attracted to her. He told me so straight out. I told him, great. I wasn't jealous. I knew I had to get away from him. I was ready to do whatever it took. At least then I was. I think he wanted to get away from me, too. He started making out with Ema all the time. Compulsively. She was so in love with him, she'd do whatever he wanted. That time you first came over, they started making out, right? He knew exactly what he was doing. He liked to do it with her in front of me. He must have been watching me, to see how I'd react. It wasn't you, you know. It was me. Always me. Again and again I had to get up and go so they could have the place to themselves. I thought it would somehow take a load off me to leave, but I only felt worse. A hundred times or more I had to watch them hug and kiss, and every time it felt like getting dragged through the mud. I don't know why. I don't think it was jealousy. If I'd been jealous, I'd never have let him get involved with her in the first place. I think I felt… lonely. That's it. What I felt was loneliness. Nothing so positive as jealousy. There was this incredible sense of loss. The way you'd feel if an identical twin you'd been raised with from birth suddenly went away… And that's when it happened, Kyoko." He crinkled his eyes and cautiously looked my way. "That's when you came along."

I thought of the rainy day in June when I'd run into Wataru and Yunosuke again in A Cappella. Yunosuke had left early, saying he had a date with Ema. Wataru and I, left to our own devices, had gone to a wine bar. He'd talked a mile a minute, bringing up topic after topic. I can't remember all he said, but he was voluble and animated, and there was no stopping him. That was the day I fell in love with him. That same day he'd been suffering inside, aching from a need for Yunosuke that he could neither satisfy nor ignore. While I'd fluttered with excitement at a vague promise of romance, he'd sat there with his thoughts on a completely different plane, restless and prattling blindly on to mask his pain and ambivalence.

I'd lost him from the very start, I thought. I'd never had him to begin with. So what was this enormous sense of loss? An amputated limb goes right on hurting, I remembered hearing somewhere. A part of you that's not even there goes on causing pain and discomfort. Was that what I felt now, nothing but phantom pain?

Wataru went on. "Things started up naturally with you, I think. You may think otherwise, but that's how it seemed to me. Little by little… yeah, really little by little… I felt myself opening up to you emotionally. You were so much fun to be with. You acted so grown up, but you came from a sheltered background, and there was a sweet innocence about you; sometimes you'd act tough, but that only drew me in more. This may sound funny, but... I made a conscious decision to love you. I thought I could. I was quite confident – and I *did*. That's the thing. I got so wrapped up in how I felt that I never stopped to think about how *he* felt. When he and I were alone together, we never talked about you or her. For the last two years, we pretended to be ordinary buddies. After a while, we didn't have to pretend. That's what we were, just a couple of guys who happened to be friends. So that day when it snowed and you caught him looking in at us, I was shocked. I know you were shocked too, but I bet I was more than you. I felt as if I'd seen right down into his heart. I never wanted to. I knew that if we only went on the way we were, we'd both make it through. But then he came and saw us together, and I saw into his heart. So we landed right back where we started."

Still leaning against the stereo, I touched my cheek. The room was stifling, but I didn't feel like getting up and opening a window. My cheek felt sticky, I was sweating so much.

Wataru quietly cleared his throat, and swallowed. "To tell the truth, it made me happy that he was jealous. Seeing how jealous he was of you and me made me happier than I can say."

He closed his mouth at that point, took a deep breath and swept his hair back. "I didn't mean to break our date tonight. I was looking forward to spending the night with you here. But... something went off the rails. I got mixed up. For two years Yunosuke and I were friends, and then just like that, we were back. I can't explain what happened after that. Even if I could... it would only make things worse."

Fresh tears started in my eyes as I sat on the floor with my arms around my knees. In my frazzled mind rose Ema's face. Ema, who knew nothing. Were she and I victims? Girls unknowingly used by gay lovers as a cover? Or were we the ones at fault, a pair of naive intruders who tried to break up the relationship between two men?

I wiped my nose and looked at him. From the bed he stretched out a pale, delicate hand to me. I felt as if my hand was being drawn into his, but I couldn't move. Still reaching out to me, he slipped down from the bed and came over beside me. His hand moved up my bare arm, and then around my shoulders.

"Tell me something," I said.

His hand stopped, like a blotter on my sweaty skin. I tilted my head to look at him.

"What do I do now?"

His face, close to mine, seemed misty, as if in a haze. He smelled faintly of rain. Quietly he said, "That's for you to decide, Kyoko."

That answer was a last stake of ice in my heart. It finalized everything. I held my breath, feeling the blood pound in my temples, and bit hard on the inside of my cheek. Wataru's beautiful face grew dim, swayed, and blurred.

That's for you to decide, Kyoko.

How could I possibly decide a thing like that? I was an ordinary girl fresh out of high school, going on nineteen, studying for her college exams, that's all. I could barely comprehend the reality of two men loving each other in the first place; how was I supposed to force them apart, compel one of them to turn to me? It was beyond my powers. I wasn't a man, I was a woman. And for that reason alone, Wataru would forever see me as someone from a different world. I couldn't change that.

For a second I glimpsed the endless stretch of blank, featureless time that would begin after we broke up. It was like a stretch of water, a fetid dull gray. I didn't know which way I was headed anymore. I was stranded in the middle of a vast and empty space.

"But I loved you," I murmured. "I loved you so much." The tears wouldn't stop coming; I couldn't breathe. Wataru held me close. I buried my face in his shirt that smelled of rain, and wept.

Outside, raindrops dripped from the eaves. The wind and rain had died down.

10

Tchaikovsky was gay, they say. After hearing Wataru's confession, I reread the jacket blurb to the Pathétique and noticed the word "homosexual" there for the first time. This was nearly ten months after Wataru had given me the record for my birthday. Though I'd read the commentary several times, somehow I'd persistently overlooked that word. It was in a passing reference to the question of why his Symphony No. 6 was called "Pathétique": "As neither Tchaikovsky himself nor anyone close to him ever offered any explanation, a host of conflicting theories developed, including the notion that the title expressed the pain of being homosexual." One brief sentence, raising and dismissing the hypothesis as if it were something that lowered the cachet of Tchaikovsky's music.

Had Wataru given me this to read in hope that I would pick up on it? Had he been trying to tell me something? Or was it only coincidence?

I listened to the symphony over and over again. I heard it so many times that even now, twenty years on, its haunting melodies are fixed in my mind.

After his confession, I often wondered how the two of them spent their time together. What did they do? What was their day like? As far as I know, the student movement put Tohoku University out of commission. It may have been only natural that I never heard either of them talk about the place, but even so they seemed a race apart, ignoring the usual student activities.

I tried to picture how they lived, never going to classes and having no social life to speak of, but I had trouble coming up with a realistic image. What time in the morning did they get up? Ten? They were a pair of night owls, so it might have been later. When they did get up, which one made the instant coffee? Neither of them was very interested in food, so it's possible they ate nothing solid for breakfast. If they did, it was probably a slice of stale bread. Or maybe they shared a leftover doughnut from the day before.

After breakfast, what would they have done? Listen to records. Clean up a little. Read, or maybe go for a walk. They both lived on an allowance from home, so sometimes they must have gone out to pick up cash, or to phone for more money. But they wouldn't do that every day. So how did they spend the long afternoons?

When they eventually tired of their cramped quarters they probably went into town. Pushed open the door to A Cappella, killed a few hours there. Then Ema would drop by, or me. We two must have been terrific time-killers for them. They made a habit of this, two couples passing the time of day together.

Apparently, Ema and Yunosuke had frequent sex in the teahouse, but seldom spent the night together. Most evenings it would have been just him and Wataru again. What did they do then? Read, listen to music, carry on desultory conversations, read some more. Listen to more music, have more snatches of conversation. How did they get to the public bath? Did they walk there together, one of them carrying a plastic bucket and two towels as they ducked under the dark blue curtain at the entrance?

The teahouse was always piled with books, I remember, but no specific titles come to mind. The place was buried in books and records and cigarette butts. Apart from scribbling some sort of prose and seeing an occasional movie, they had no particular interests. Neither of them was the type to get absorbed in a hobby. They didn't work, they didn't study, and few of the pleasures the world had to offer seemed to appeal to them. What were they all about? Did they focus entirely on one another?

Perhaps at bedtime they exchanged a kiss or held hands. Wataru told me that for two years they'd lived together as platonic friends. What was there to back up his claim, to make me believe it? I didn't know. In all that time was there truly never a goodnight kiss, never an unconscious caress in sleep, never the slight tension of the moment when one slipped into bed with the other in search of warmth?

But more than the thought of any physical contact, what aroused my fiercest jealousy was the thought that, even as they held themselves back, they must have felt persistent pangs of longing for each other.

This drove me nearly to distraction. Next to that constant yearning, I thought, what were a hundred acts of "perversion"? The two of them had stayed celibate while waiting, all along, for the inevitable explosion of desire. Ema and I were just props serving a temporary purpose.

The word "platonic" was misleading, I felt. When two people of any gender try to suppress their mutual physical desire, they inevitably engage in mental sex. It was this, too – the thought of the fantasies taking place between them – that tortured me more than the physical act. Yunosuke and Wataru were emotionally and mentally making out. While sleeping with Ema and me, in the dark they had mind-fucked each other, had had sex that was infinitely weirder and more erotic.

After spending the night of the typhoon with Wataru, I wrote to him several times only to rip up what I'd written and start again. It was a good ten days before I came up with a letter that I could bear to send.

In it I expressed my feelings as honestly and calmly as I could. I told him that I was still getting over the shock. That it would take time, but since no greater shock could lie in the offing, eventually I was bound to recover. All I could do was wait for time to pass. I couldn't go on seeing him as before, but even so my feelings for him would never change, and knowing this was what caused the greatest pain.

At the end I added that I didn't want to see him for a month. Of all the things I wrote, that was the one and only lie. I could barely make it through a single day without him. Together, we would only rehash the same old things, and my confusion would only deepen. Still, I had no idea how I was going to get along without him.

I did all I could to put on a bold front. I didn't have it in me to go on seeking his affection day after day when he'd come straight out and told me he was in love with someone else – Yunosuke, of all people. Only a bold front would save me. That's what I believed.

Wataru's answer was delivered to my aunt's mailbox a week later. In flowing characters down the middle of a sheet of notebook paper he had written, "I'll wait as long as you want, Kyoko, until you feel ready. See you in October. I miss you." That was all. Below his signature he had scribbled a sentence in English, in tiny lettering: "*I am a fool.*"

I stopped studying. I still went to class, but the teachers' words no longer registered. My score in the practice test was abysmal. My memory began slipping, and my powers of concentration were shot. My mind fogged over. Colors grew faint, until everything was the grainy gray of an old black and white movie.

Pretending for my aunt's sake that life was going on as usual was extremely difficult. We were together only at mealtimes, but the mere effort of responding to her chatter or laughing at the appropriate places in a TV show wore me out. After dinner I would head straight for my room and sit at my desk staring blankly at the wall, with books and notebooks spread out in case she came in with tea. Sometimes I sat like this until it started to grow light outside.

I never felt the urge to talk things over with anyone. I couldn't see how to do it. Getting advice about exams or friendships or an ordinary broken heart was one thing, but who would lend an ear to a teenage girl whose boyfriend was gay? I doubt that any of my friends back then could have come up with a reasoned opinion. Grownups – people supposedly wiser in the ways of the world – would react in an all too predictable way. Their eyes would widen in appalled surprise and they would ply me with questions, full of keen interest, until their curiosity was satisfied. Then, inwardly planning with excitement who to tell this grotesque story to first, they would advise me – almost as an afterthought – to break up with him.

But that wasn't what I wanted to know. Neither did I need a Freudian analysis of the homosexual male. It was about myself I wanted to know more. I wanted to know why, although my gender ruled out any chance of reestablishing a real connection with him, I still hungered for him and wanted to be with him. Absurd as it was, I cursed myself for being female, cursed him for being male – and, most of all, cursed the stars that had made Yunosuke male, too.

And so September went by. All I can remember now is the shift my feelings underwent in that month. That and one other thing: one afternoon after it had stopped raining, I was playing in the yard with Mogu when I was bitten by some kind of poisonous insect, and developed a huge boil on my right ankle. It got infected and wouldn't heal. When I put on a sock, the pain made me jump. My

aunt urged me to see a doctor, but I wouldn't go. I didn't want to talk
to anyone I didn't have to, not even a doctor.

About the time the boil drained and the swelling went down, I
sent Wataru a brief note care of Yunosuke at the Kitayama address:
"It's October. Let me know when and where I can see you."

The answer came, to my surprise, by telephone. My aunt was busy
giving a piano lesson, so I took the call.

"Thanks for the card," he said. "That was a long month. Way
longer than I thought it would be."

I took a deep breath. Managing with effort to keep my voice
steady, I replied, "Same here. How've you been?"

"Not so great, actually. How about you?"

"Me neither." I was about to ask how Yunosuke was, but bit my
tongue. I didn't have the courage to mention his name. Instead I said,
"I haven't seen Setsuko for ages. How's she doing?"

"I saw her a week ago. She's fine. Helping out at the store now,
part-time. She says she's a real hit with the customers."

"Oh yeah?" I said, and smiled. "You know, I can just see her in a
kimono, selling those old-fashioned sweets. It would suit her. Like
something in a movie. That's great."

"Think so?" he said.

There was a short silence. I moistened my lips and gripped the
receiver tighter.

He said, "I'm thinking that I would like to make a date to see you
next Saturday afternoon in the teahouse." It sounded as if he were
translating an English sentence into Japanese, with awkward pauses.
"How about it?"

"In Kitayama?"

"Yeah. But not if you'd rather not."

"I don't mind. It's just…"

"Yunosuke won't be there," he said noncommittally. "He's leaving
for Tokyo that morning, so the place'll be empty. If that's okay."

"I'll be there," I told him.

"Good," he said, adding, "I read your letter again and again. I was
happy you wrote."

After we hung up I went out into the yard. It was a bright, peaceful
day. Signs of the coming of fall were everywhere. Mogu ran up to me,

and I patted his head and hugged his firm brown body. There was the smell of dog, the smell of earth, the smell of sunshine. Listening to a piano student stumble through a Czerny *étude*, I buried my face in the fur on Mogu's back.

That Saturday at exactly one in the afternoon I slipped through the hole in the hedge by the teahouse. After a night's rain the ferns by the hedge and stepping-stones were a luxuriant green. I was so nervous that my knees shook, but I commanded myself not to think about it. Dwelling on the past was a waste of time. If you didn't have the courage to sift through what had happened and make peace with it somehow, you shouldn't pretend otherwise. *Go with the flow.*

I moved slowly over the stepping-stones and looked up at the bamboo grove where leaves stirred noiselessly in the clear autumn sunshine. Beyond was the dark roof of the teahouse. It was right there, just as ever.

Then I came to a sudden stop. In front of the teahouse stood Ema. She was wearing a mustard-colored turtleneck and a black miniskirt with black lace-up boots. As I approached she was chewing gum hard and looking off into the distance, unaware of me.

Twenty years on, I can still see her standing there. She was leaning against the wall next to the crawl-in entrance with her arms folded casually, her long slim legs crossed. She was carrying a brown knit shoulder bag that swung back and forth to the rhythm of her chewing.

I remember her pose so well, not only because it looked so cool and sophisticated – she was dressed with such flair that she might have stepped out of a fashion magazine – No, but because something about her was different. I don't quite know how to put it. Maybe I imagined it, but she seemed to have a newly practical, down-to-earth look. If she'd suddenly slipped into an apron and started folding laundry in the sunny corner of a little apartment, humming to herself, it would have suited her perfectly. That's what I mean.

Sensing my presence, she turned towards me with a start. Her curved, pencil-thin eyebrows went up in surprise, and she broke into a smile. "Well, look who's here!" she said. "Long time no see. Where the hell have you been keeping yourself?" She ran up to me, her big breasts swaying under her sweater like soft fruit. "I called you so many times. That scary aunt of yours always answered the phone and said you were busy studying."

This was news to me. All I said was, "Sorry." Presumably, my aunt had thought we would spend too long on the phone, and purposely refrained from telling me she'd called. Still, if I'd ever answered the phone myself, I would have been at a loss to know what to say.

"Were you really studying the whole time?" she asked teasingly.

I nodded vaguely.

"You weren't talking to Wataru either, apparently. I worried about you, wondering what you were up to."

"Nobody home?" I asked, pointing to the teahouse. The door was shut tight.

She shook her head glumly. "You know what Yunosuke did? Went off to Tokyo without even telling me. When I got here a minute ago, I found a note saying he'd left. What a letdown. I didn't feel like turning around and going straight home, so I was just standing here doing nothing. I'm glad I got to see you. You waiting for Wataru?"

"We were supposed to meet here. Where could he have gone?"

"Who knows? I bet he'll be right back. Probably went out shopping or something. If you wait, he'll show up. Want to go inside?"

I demurred. "It's nicer out here."

"Right," she said, snapping her gum. There was a whiff of strawberry in the air. "I'll wait with you. Nothing better to do."

We talked in snatches as we strolled around. She jumped from stepping-stone to stepping-stone like a child, sniffed the vegetation, and looked up at the sky, until she grew bored and leaned against the old stone lantern at the border between the main house and the garden.

"Kyoko, can I bum a cigarette?" she asked.

I nodded, pulled a pack of MF out of my bag and handed it to her with a book of matches. She said thanks and lit up with a practiced hand.

"Smoking while you chew gum tastes surprisingly good." She exhaled a lungful of smoke with evident pleasure. "It's probably all in my mind, but I feel like the nicotine content gets reduced, so it's not as bad for me."

I laughed. "Worrying about your health while you smoke? That's a good one. Your lungs are coal black anyway, you can count on it. The only way to fix them now would be to open you up in an operating room, take them out and scrub them clean with detergent."

"I know it," she said. "I'm just starting to get in maternal mode."

I looked at her. Leaning against the tall lantern, she giggled. A dry autumn breeze gently scattered the smoke from her cigarette.

"I'm pregnant," she said, looking at me. "I hadn't had my period in the longest time, so I went to the hospital to be sure… I'm already three months gone, they said."

Her big eyes stared straight at me, moistened, shone, and blinked with happiness. I couldn't speak. My lips were probably trembling.

She tilted her head to one side and smiled mischievously. "Nothing to be so surprised about, silly. Don't just stand there with your mouth open – tell me you're happy for me. I'm having Yunosuke's baby!"

"You mean… you're really… going to have it?" My voice was hoarse.

"Of course," she said emphatically, and took a drag on her cigarette. "Why wouldn't I?"

"What did Yunosuke say?"

"'Get rid of it.' You know him, he hates kids. But I told him nothing doing. Just for the record, it's not because I'm against abortion or anything like that. Respect for life isn't something I've ever really thought about much. Unwanted children shouldn't be brought into the world if you ask me, and if I'd gotten pregnant with any other guy, I'd have headed straight for a clinic. But this is special. I've wanted Yunosuke's baby for the longest time, more than anything else. I thought I'd wait 'til I finished high school, anyway, but now that I have, why wait? The due date is next May. I'll be a college student and a mom at the same time."

It wasn't a cold day. The breeze had a slight edge to it but the sun was warm, everything was pleasantly dry, and the air I breathed in was redolent of fall. Yet I was covered in gooseflesh. I felt sick, the way you do when you get a noseful of something rotten.

I was torn. What should I do, blurt out the truth there and then? Tell her it was Wataru that Yunosuke loved, that she was nothing more to him than a sort of pet, someone with whom he could test his masculinity? Tell her straight out that the man she loved was gay?

"Come on, Kyoko," she said, laughing with amusement and poking me in the arm. "There's no reason to look so worried.

I'm fine! Yunosuke and I will make a go of it. There's nothing to be afraid of."

I reached out and laid a hand on the mossy lantern to support my suddenly wobbly knees. "What do you mean, make a go of it? You mean you're going to get married?"

"Well, yeah."

"Has he proposed?"

"No." She puffed out her cheeks in slight discontent. She must have thought I was going to say something annoyingly old-fashioned. "He hates the very word 'marriage.' He doesn't like it when people get all romantic about what's really just a piece of paper. Of course I'm the same way. You are too, aren't you, Kyoko?"

I stammered something and nodded quickly.

Ema shook her boyishly cut hair. "Anyway, the two of us will make it work. I mean, I'm having his baby. What other choice is there? I sure don't want to raise a baby all by myself. I won't be able to work for a while, for one thing. I'll need his help. He hasn't ever sat down with me and laid out his plans for the future in so many words, but I know he's thinking hard about it. He's a serious person."

A breeze sprang up and swayed a maple tree whose leaves were just beginning to change color. A single leaf floated down and danced over our heads before flitting behind the teahouse.

The devil inside me raised its head, and with a smirk began to whisper. To keep Ema from noticing, I leaned back against the stone lantern and closed my eyes.

Say nothing. That's what the devil whispered. Since Ema was determined to have this baby, why not keep quiet, let her have her way? Yunosuke might be gay, but he was clearly capable of loving a woman, too. Now that he'd got her pregnant, like it or not he'd have to face the future. This might be just what it took for him to break up with Wataru. At the very least, the question of what to do about the baby would create a rift between them, that much was certain. I would use Ema and the baby she was carrying to pry Wataru away from Yunosuke. Tear down the world the two of them had built up. Why bother to tell Ema the absurd truth? This was my chance. She had created this chance for me.

"Such a pretty day," she said lazily. "You know something? Ever since I found out about the baby, things like a pretty day or the smell of the wind – ordinary little things like that – really get to me. You'll understand when you get pregnant, someday, Kyoko. Every little thing affects you."

I turned and looked at her. She'd slipped a hand under her miniskirt waistband and was stroking her still-flat belly, smiling serenely. The wind stirred incessantly, rustling the trees around us.

"When I start to show I'll leave home. I haven't told my parents yet. They'd have a heart attack. It makes me feel bad, but what can I do? Next year I'll be twenty, anyway – a legal adult. And it's my decision."

"I'll help you out," I said cheerfully. The devil inside me applauded. *That's the way, keep it up.* I put on my best smile, turned to her and held out a hand. "Congrats," I said. "I feel happy, too."

She pressed my cold hand lightly and said a shy thanks, adding, "I wish you and Wataru all the luck, too."

I acknowledged this with a grunt and a nod. Then I felt someone's presence at a distance, and turned to see Wataru slowly crossing the stepping-stones, making his way towards us. When he caught sight of us, he called out with a smile, "Sorry! I went out shopping."

"There, see?" laughed Ema. "Told you so."

In the month since I'd last seen him, Wataru had grown thinner and even better looking. He glanced at me bashfully and said in a quiet voice, "Long time no see." I nodded.

"Well, I'll be going," said Ema, but she lingered, kicking dirt with the toe of her boot. Plainly, she wanted to be asked to stay. I thought, *I'll use her,* God help me, that's what I thought.

"Why not stay and have a cup of coffee? Okay, Wataru?"

He seemed rather taken aback that I didn't want to be alone with him, but he didn't show it openly. "Absolutely," he said. "I got some apples. We can have those, too."

The three of us went inside, and while I boiled some water and made coffee for us, Ema peeled an apple and arranged the slices on a plate. Just as I knew she would, she began to tell Wataru her big news. I kept a close watch on his expression, which never wavered – a sign in itself of the impact it made.

When Ema then started to change the subject, I deliberately asked questions that got her back on track. This delighted her. Before long she was talking frankly about the particular session with Yunosuke that had probably resulted in conception. On and on she went about that early summer afternoon in the teahouse: how long his ejaculation had been, how much pleasure she'd felt, everything.

"...Like the door to my womb was opening – Kyoko, you know what I mean? That's just how it felt. I thought, *this could be it*. I could feel the door opening and his sperm shooting through it into a tiny passageway that went deeper and deeper inside me, spreading out until it was like my whole body filled up with his sperm. I think that was it – the moment I conceived. I'm sure of it..."

Wataru was leaning an elbow on the windowsill, looking out. His face was expressionless. I could see at a glance that he had pulled down a shutter inside him, trying to keep from listening. I felt triumphant.

Oblivious, Ema kept chattering on about conception, pregnancy, childbirth, and other aspects of reproduction. She stayed 'til evening. After she left Wataru and I went for a walk around the local temple grounds. While the treetops swayed in the autumn wind, I cautiously linked my arm in his and put my lips to his ear.

"It's okay now," I said. "I brooded about things until I didn't even know what I was thinking anymore. But it's okay now. Everything's okay, just the way it is."

He was silent. I kept on talking.

"Ema's news was a shock, I bet."

He smiled meaninglessly and came to a standstill. There in the twilight among the trees, his arms circled me in a light embrace. I smelled his familiar smell and drew it deep into my lungs, simultaneously despising and blessing the devil inside me. *This is what you have to do to live*, I thought. *Sometimes you've got to steal the one you love. It's how life is.*

"I love you, Wataru," I whispered.

"Me too," he said.

Standing on the dry ground with our arms around each other, we brushed lips in a kiss as light as a butterfly landing on a petal. Then I bit his lips, forced them apart. For a second he stiffened as if in consternation, before sucking greedily on mine.

The next month, on November 25th, the writer Yukio Mishima committed suicide by ritual disembowelment at the army headquarters in Ichigaya, Tokyo. I heard about it in study hall. Everyone got very excited, and some people ran outside in tears. That night, after my aunt and I watched the news on TV, I stayed in my room and reread the Mishima paperback I'd bought. While I read, I played the Pathétique.

Just three weeks later, after school on December 15th, the phone rang. My aunt answered it. It was around four in the afternoon, I'm pretty sure. I was washing my hands when she called out, "It's for you." I wiped my hands on a towel and asked loudly, "Who is it?" She didn't answer.

When I went to the living room, she was standing with her hand over the receiver, shaking her head. "I don't know who it is. The name is Domoto, but it's a woman."

Setsuko, I thought. I took the receiver from her outstretched hand. I'd given Setsuko my aunt's phone number, but this was the first time she'd ever called. As I put the receiver to my ear, I caught a whiff of camphor from my aunt's kimono. It stung my nostrils like an omen.

"Hello?" said Setsuko. "Kyoko?" Her voice was unusually sad and subdued. My eyes were focused on some tangerines in the living room. They were piled high in a basket, and rays of winter sunshine cast striped shadows across them. "I just heard from the police," said Setsuko, and lowered her voice still more. "Your friend Ema... Ema Takamiya... has been murdered."

The pattern of stripes on the tangerines fell apart. I screamed hysterically. My aunt came running. "Ema's been murdered. Ema's been murdered." I shouted the words over and over like an idiot.

11

There was no discrepancy between my aunt's testimony and mine. That's because on December 14th, the day Ema was killed, Wataru came over for dinner and the three of us sat around together 'til nine sharp. She and I both saw him to the door, and he thanked her for the meal. I remember that he wondered aloud about the bus, and we both said, "There'll be one at 9:10."

Seizing the chance to be alone with Wataru even for a few minutes, I walked him down to the end of the lane. It had snowed all day, but by then it had stopped. Side by side, we picked our way through the white drifts in the lane. We stopped in the shadow of a telephone pole at the corner, and I lifted my face for his goodnight kiss. Just then a bicycle came out of nowhere and slammed on its brakes in front of us. The high school girl from the house on the corner got off her bike and came towards us in surprise.

Hastily I pulled away from him and greeted her in a purposely loud voice. She said hi, looking from my face to his with keen interest.

That was shortly after nine o'clock, as her testimony later confirmed. She had gone to her grandmother's house for a visit, but left because she wanted to see a TV show that started at nine. Her grandmother felt that TV was a bad influence, so rather than asking to see it she hurried home in time to watch the show. She testified that she arrived home "around nine o'clock... no more than a minute or two past the hour, for sure."

Whether Wataru had indeed been in my aunt's home until nine o'clock on the evening of December 14th was to be a focal point of the investigation. The reliability of his later "confession" hinged on the question of his alibi.

Ema's body was found early on the morning of the fifteenth in a corner of the Rinnoji temple compound. The head priest found her and notified the police right away. She was found lying face up at the foot of a tree with her hands crossed on her chest. Her plaid pleated skirt was pressed close to her legs, and her eyes were shut. She lay there so neatly that the priest said at first he thought someone had thrown away a newish mannequin.

Beside her body was a shoulder bag containing a makeup kit, a red wallet, a rail pass holder, a handkerchief, and some gum. Instead of a rail pass, the holder contained a student ID card from her women's college, a book of bus tickets, and a piece of paper with a few telephone numbers, including those of Setsuko Domoto, my aunt, and several of Ema's high school and college friends. Since Setsuko's name topped the list, the police lost no time in notifying her of Ema's death and saying they wanted to ask some questions. At that point they were unaware of the existence of Yunosuke and Wataru. Right after Setsuko's phone call, they called my aunt's number. I was too upset to remember, but my aunt says she took the call.

A quick autopsy was done, and strangulation was established as the cause of death. The time of death was thought to be somewhere between eight and nine o'clock on the evening of the fourteenth. As the soles of her boots bore no traces of soil or snow from the temple compound and there was no sign of a struggle, the police proceeded on the assumption that she had been strangled elsewhere and left in the compound.

Near the body was a suspicious set of footprints. Because the snow had fallen all afternoon and stopped in the evening, they were easy to distinguish. They were made by a pair of men's sneakers, size ten.

My reaction, of course, had been shock, that this happened to someone I knew so well, though compared to what came later, her death seems almost secondary. Without time to absorb it, I was summoned to the police station and questioned in detail. Who had Ema Takamiya been seeing? Did she have more than one boyfriend? How well did I know her? The last time I saw her, what did we talk about? She was pregnant – did I know that? Did I have any idea who the father might be?

Ironically, after Ema died I realized just how alone in life she was, how few friends she ever had. The police checked out her other acquaintances and came up with almost nothing. All they had to go on was Setsuko's and my testimony. Apart from Setsuko, Ema's closest friend had been me. She'd seemed so outgoing, so likely to easily make friends – yet she'd lived and died alone, telling no one but me about Yunosuke.

I was so tense that I suddenly felt woozy, ran to the toilet and threw up my breakfast. The police officers said it was only natural. They expressed sympathy: here I was studying hard for entrance exams and a friend of mine got murdered.

I wasn't the only one who mentioned Yunosuke's name as Ema's boyfriend. Setsuko also told them what she knew, naturally. How could we do otherwise? Wataru, the only other person who knew the ins and outs of their relationship, had been missing since the night of the murder and could not be reached for questioning.

Both Yunosuke and Wataru had disappeared. It drove me crazy. From the very beginning I'd suspected Yunosuke was the murderer. I knew it instinctively the moment Setsuko broke the news. I knew why Wataru had gone missing, too.

After Setsuko and I both gave Yunosuke's name, the police wasted no time in following it up. As well they might. The child Ema had been carrying was supposedly his, and even if she had made the story up, once I told them about our conversation, suspicion had naturally fallen on him.

The police were interested to learn that Yunosuke had a roommate who was my boyfriend and Setsuko's younger brother, but Wataru was never on their list of suspects. At the time of Ema's murder he'd been with me, for one thing, and he had no discernible motive. His disappearance after the incident was not viewed as particularly significant. Yunosuke was the one they were after.

For as long as I live I will never forget how the day of December 14th started and ended. In the morning, sunlight had straggled between the clouds, but around noon the sky suddenly filled with snow and it turned cold. I had one class in the morning and one in the afternoon; after it started to snow I stayed on for a bit. I'd made little headway in my studies, but with entrance exams just a couple of months off I had to do what I could.

My decision to go on seeing Wataru had brought me out of the worst of my slump. Next on my agenda was to get into college, get myself to Tokyo, and then by travelling back and forth between

Tokyo and Sendai, work on building our relationship into something stronger. I thought of nothing else.

Ema was by then five months along, but not showing much, partly because she was pretty well endowed to begin with. Only the keenest observer would have guessed. What private discussions Yunosuke and Wataru may have had about her impending motherhood I don't know, but Wataru made it sound as if Yunosuke had decided to respect her decision to give birth. I never really believed it. It seemed unlikely to me that he would come to terms with the situation that easily. It would have been far more like him to drag her off to a clinic for an abortion, but I gave little thought to his failure to do that, either. Basically, I didn't care what happened to either of them. As long as he was made to fulfill his obligation to her in some fashion, leaving Wataru alone, I'd be happy.

Ema hadn't yet told her parents about the baby. She said she was going to make a clean breast of it at New Year's. There was no particular reason why it had to be then. I think that to her, telling her parents meant moving out of their home; she saw it as a kind of formality. That was the only reason for picking New Year's Day.

When the time came, she intended to move into the teahouse. Just as I wasn't thinking seriously about her, neither did she have Wataru's interests at heart. She probably figured that since he had family close by, he could always go and stay with them. This was perfect for my purposes. I told her emphatically that I thought it was a fine idea. Once she moved in, Wataru would have no choice but to move out. Like it or not, he would have to distance himself from Yunosuke.

I hadn't laid eyes on Yunosuke since the summer night when I'd stumbled on the two of them locked passionately together. I'm sure he wanted to see me even less than I wanted to see him. Word of him came to me indirectly, through Ema and Wataru, but I paid little attention to what they said. I wanted to wipe out the very thought of him. As time went by and things changed, it was inevitable that Wataru would leave him and come to me. That's what I wanted to believe. I was more than half persuaded that Wataru loved me. Like a fool, somewhere inside I believed that same-sex love couldn't possibly compare in depth to the love between a man and a woman.

That day, I left class sometime after four thirty in the afternoon. I had no plans to see Wataru, but neither did I feel like going straight home. I wandered through the streets in the falling snow, looking in store windows and browsing at a boutique that sold cheap little things before heading into A Cappella. Inside were Wataru and Yunosuke, with Ema.

"The four of us are together again!" she exclaimed gaily, and so the awkwardness between Yunosuke and me passed unnoticed.

I remember exactly what she was wearing: a warm-looking plaid pleated skirt, lace-up boots and a white sweater. She'd given up smoking and coffee and was virtuously drinking tea with lemon. I smiled at her and said, "So how's it going? Everything okay?"

She held up two fingers in a V sign and said, "Absolutely." She didn't look pregnant at all. In my complete innocence of the physical changes caused by pregnancy – something I could then only imagine – it seemed unbelievable that she should be out on the town as usual, sitting with a smile on her face, drinking tea.

Yunosuke was in a surprisingly good mood, as far as I could tell. In fact he seemed so animated that Wataru beside him was rather eclipsed. Feeling a bit catty, I said, "Hey, congratulations! This time next year, you'll be a father." As soon as I'd spoken I felt sick at my own meanness. But Yunosuke, unfazed, only gave a small chuckle.

After that there was no more mention of Ema's baby. We stayed on safe, inoffensive topics and chattered away like any group of chums, our laughter sometimes becoming so boisterous that the waiters frowned.

Wataru showed consideration for my feelings by avoiding speaking directly to Yunosuke and addressing his remarks to me. He was like any person who, finding himself seated by a former lover, gives all his attention to his current lover to reassure her. All perfectly ordinary.

In their company, it began to seem as if what I'd seen on the night of the storm was only a bad dream. Everyone was so completely normal: the lovebirds who, though they'd become expectant parents a little too early, had resolved to stay together; the high school graduate studying for college entrance exams, and her attentive boyfriend.

After the better part of an hour, Yunosuke whispered something to Ema, and she glowed and nodded. "Sorry, you two," he said. "We're going to take off a little early."

Wataru looked at Yunosuke, but Yunosuke didn't return the look. His eyes were on me. "We've got somewhere to go."

"By all means," I said boldly. "Don't worry about us, we'll be fine." *Just go away and stay away*, I wanted to say. I intended my remark to drip with sarcasm, but Yunosuke seemed not to notice.

Ema said, "See you, then," looking at Wataru and me in turn, and got up. "Let's get together again soon. All four of us."

"You take care of yourself," I told her. "Watch your step, don't fall."

"I've got a strong arm to lean on here, so I'll be fine," she said, beaming and holding tight to Yunosuke.

Wataru and I laughed automatically.

They put on their coats and got up to go. Albinoni's "Adagio" was playing. A group of high school students sat in front of the huge speakers at one end of the room; the air was a mauve haze of cigarette smoke. The hem of Ema's pleated skirt disappeared out the door. After they were gone, I stared on and on at the closed door.

Wataru seemed fidgety, far less at ease than when Yunosuke had been there. But that was something I didn't realize 'til later, looking back. At the time I wasn't really paying attention.

"I never thought the four of us would get together again," I said with studied casualness. "It was kind of weird."

He nodded and stuck a cigarette in his mouth. His big, liquid dark eyes focused on me. "Funny," he said.

"What?"

The sweet sound of the Adagio hung like a membrane between us. After staring at me for a moment, he slowly lit his cigarette with a match. While he exhaled smoke I watched his lips.

"It seemed funny from the beginning. Why didn't you tell Ema?"

"Tell her what?" I said, deliberately obtuse.

Skewing the corners of his mouth in a grimace, he let out a silent sigh as if to expel some unspoken pain. "I was quite sure you would. I wasn't the only one, either – Yunosuke thought so too. We both thought that surely, with the way things were, you'd—"

"I can't," I interrupted him quietly. "I'm never telling anyone. Ever."

He nodded, and his lips curved faintly. "No ordinary girl, this."

"Not true," I said, working up a grin. "I'm as ordinary as they come."

156

He looked at me with a melancholy smile. For a time we sat motionless, looking into each other's eyes.

I had grown used to the tension-filled silences between us, but for some reason the silence of that moment was unnerving. It occurred to me that perhaps my sinister plan – to say nothing to Ema about the secret, and use her pregnancy to pry Wataru and Yunosuke apart – was an open book to him.

"You wanted me to tell her?" To calm my nerves, I gave him a pouty smile. "If you want her to know so much, why not just tell her yourself? Wild horses won't drag it out of me."

"That's not the point," he said, barely moving his lips. "Don't get me wrong. I don't want to tell her, either."

"You know perfectly well why I haven't said anything."

"Yeah, I do," he said, his tone matter of fact.

"Sometimes people are better off not knowing things," I said with a know-it-all air, and nodded to myself. "Besides, she's happy now."

"Right. I think so too," said Wataru, and looked away.

For a while longer we sat in silence, smoking. Then we stubbed out our cigarettes and left. Outside, the snow had stopped.

We went out arm in arm. For once Wataru didn't take me to the bus stop. Instead we went to the park, where we walked around the deserted, frozen fountain before heading towards my aunt's house. It was a long time since he'd walked me home. He asked me several times if I was cold, and when he realized my cheeks were icy, he took off his white wool muffler and wrapped it around my lower face.

When we turned right into a quiet residential area, just one block away from my aunt's house, I couldn't stand it anymore and came to a stop. Walking down a snow-dusted sidewalk in the freezing cold, with the arm of the person I cared about most in the world wrapped snugly around my shoulders, how could I maintain my composure?

"Give Yunosuke up." I looked up at him and kept my eyes fixed on him while I went on. "He's Ema's now. She's having his baby, too. Even if you went on caring for him, nothing can ever come of it now. Isn't that true?"

My heart pounded with anticipation and anxiety as I waited for his answer, eyes on his lips. In that frozen, solitary world the sound of our footsteps had ceased. All sounds had ceased.

"Give him up," I implored. I was going for broke. "It's time to decide, to choose one or the other. A or B. You can't just go on the same old way. You know that, don't you, Wataru?"

"Yeah, I know," he said quietly. His voice was so quiet that it seemed to be swallowed up in the snow.

All at once his arms were around me, holding me tight, and his lips were pressed against my cold hair. From a distance came the sound of a car passing slowly with chains on its tires. Eyes open, I buried my face in his coat. I felt only the old, familiar helplessness. My mind was empty. I wanted to cry, but no tears came.

"I trust you, Wataru," I said. "Don't ever forget that." It sounded like a line from some comic book romance or a novel for young adults. I raised my face and bit my lip.

Letting out his breath in a sigh, he said, "I won't."

Which way did we take home? Until we turned into the lane by my aunt's house, we said little. When we reached the doorstep, there was someone there. It was her.

"Welcome back," she said. In her hands was a bamboo broom, with which she had swept the snow from the concrete walkway leading to the door. The freshly swept path shone in the light from the porch as if sprinkled with granulated sugar. She looked back and forth from my face to his with frank curiosity before saying briskly, "If I let this go 'til morning, it'd freeze. I wanted to get the walk swept right away."

I looked up at Wataru uneasily, wondering what to do. I turned hesitantly to my aunt and said, "This is Wataru Domoto. He walked me home. I'm sure you remember him. Connected with Sengendo..."

Undoubtedly she had long since figured out who he was, but she registered surprise, as if understanding had just dawned. "You mean the young man we ran into that time in the department store?"

"That's right."

"The one who often phones the house?"

Wataru nodded pleasantly. "Thank you for always calling her to the phone. I apologize for the trouble."

"Not at all. You're welcome, I'm sure." Her eyes widened, the way they do when you swallow something hard, as she looked at us in turn. I could tell she'd taken a quick liking to his good looks and nice manners. Suddenly collecting herself, she said, "Dear me, here we are standing out in the freezing cold. Thank you for seeing Kyoko home. Now won't you come in and get warm?"

Wataru looked at me.

My aunt gave my arm a tug. "We're having hotpot today. Your friend hasn't eaten yet, has he? Hotpot tastes better when there are more people to share it. Why don't you ask him to stay for dinner?"

This was more than I'd bargained for. I didn't feel up to light conversation with them both over dinner.

"I have to be going," said Wataru pointedly. Perhaps because his voice was so low, however, it came out sounding rather diffident. My aunt put it down to shyness.

"You really *must* come in," she said firmly. "I've been wanting to meet you for ages. All right?"

Almost certainly the invitation seemed a nuisance to him. Yunosuke had said he and Ema had "somewhere to go" – which didn't sound like the teahouse. After seeing me home, Wataru probably meant to go back and wait up for Yunosuke. As it happens, he and Ema were already in the teahouse by then, but neither Wataru nor I had any way of knowing that.

He turned to me and said, loudly enough for my aunt to hear, "I should be going, after all."

"Honestly, it's no trouble." My aunt had already laid down the broom and stepped inside the open door. She turned back with a playful smile. "It's not like a young person to stand on ceremony. Come on in. If you go on standing in the cold that way, you'll catch your death, both of you."

Ordinarily my aunt was the austere widow dressed in a kimono, the strict piano teacher, the economizer of nunlike frugality, the determined moralist; yet she also had an artless, openhearted side, and could wangle her way with the wide-eyed innocence of an ingénue.

She didn't invite him for dinner that evening in order to pry into our relationship, of that I'm sure. I think his gallantry in escorting me home in that bitter cold made him seem like a shining knight, a fond reminder of her own youth. Her refusal to take no for an answer was tiresome, but endearing in its way.

Wataru seemed to understand this. "What do you want to do?" I murmured, and after a pause he nodded and allowed that he could stay "for an hour or so."

The table was already set, the meal ready. My aunt filled Wataru's bowl again and again with tidbits from the hotpot while chatting to him about harmless topics: my studies, the entrance exams, my parents and sister in Tokyo. He said little, but smiled often and answered her questions frankly, showing a hearty appetite as he disposed of the chunks of tofu and slices of onion and fish she pressed on him.

My aunt seemed to like him a lot – especially when she discovered he was into classical music. After dinner she plied him with tangerines while declaring that when all was said and done the best piano music was by Chopin; that to this day she still remembered clearly the words to a *canzone* she learned long ago while studying voice; that of all the songs ever written, those by Tosti were the best; that she still had dreams now and then of being seated at a grand piano in a large hall, giving a recital, and perhaps she should have become a concert pianist after all.

Wataru was the perfect listener, smiling, exclaiming, and commiserating on cue, but I could see that he was itching to get away. To stop my aunt from running on eternally, I reached under the table and pinched her surreptitiously on the knee.

"Sorry, Wataru," I said. "When she gets going on her favorite subject, there's no stopping her."

"I don't mind a bit," he said courteously. "Next time I come, I'd love to hear her play."

"Oh my," she said. "Then I must get busy and practice!"

It was then 8:50 by the living room clock. When I looked up to check the time, I exchanged a glance with Wataru, and he sent me a quiet signal. I intimated to my aunt that we should wind up this pleasant meal, and prodded Wataru. He thanked her for dinner and stood up.

Having heard that he shared lodgings with his best friend, she went to the kitchen and brought out an assortment of food – everything from canned stew and corned beef to tangerines and apples – which she proceeded to pack in a big, heavy paper bag. This took about ten minutes in all. Impatiently, I turned to her and said, "Look, loading him down with all this food is just a bother for him."

"It's nothing of the kind," she retorted. "You've never lived on your own, Kyoko, so you have no idea what it's like to scrape by. College students living away from home always complain about their food situation. There's nothing he'd rather have than something good to eat. Isn't that right, Wataru?"

He answered with a laugh, and accepted the carefully packed department store bag with a sincere thank-you. She looked obviously gratified. It pains me to think that that was the last time I ever saw him smile like this. It was a serene smile, the smile of someone at ease with himself.

After that I walked him to the end of the lane, and just as we were about to kiss goodnight, the high school girl came around the corner on her bike and saw us. So as it happened, we never got that last kiss.

Detectives determined that the size ten sneaker-prints left in the temple grounds belonged to Yunosuke Seki, and that fingerprints on the shoulder bag next to Ema's body matched prints of his taken from the teahouse. Three days after the murder, on December 17th, Yunosuke came home at one in the afternoon and surrendered peacefully to police officers who had staked the place out. He admitted to everything on the spot.

Wataru was with him then. It had been snowing all morning. After seeing him escorted away by the police, he left the teahouse and came to see me, carrying a sketchbook under one arm. It was the one he'd bought at the art supply store that time we arranged to meet there; about the size of a notebook, with stiff cardboard covers tied shut with a dark brown ribbon. The corners were curled back and the ribbon hung limply, wet from the snow. With one hand he toyed with it while he stood in the doorway and told me about Yunosuke's arrest.

"They led Yunosuke away." I think those were the exact words he used. There was even a suggestion of a smile in the curve of his mouth as he said it, his breath coming evenly. Behind him, through the open door, I could see the snow falling thickly.

As I stood there in a daze, he looked down at me and moved his mouth like he wanted to say something. I couldn't hear anything. He was there only a minute or so. He swept back his wet forelock and then went quietly away.

My aunt happened to be on the phone just then, so she never saw him. If she had, she would undoubtedly have spoken to him. What would she have said, I wonder – something vague about how sorry she was about his friend, followed by "It's cold outside, so come in and have a cup of hot tea"? She was so taken with Wataru. If things had gone differently, I think she might actually have played the piano for him.

That night he went to the police and told them that Ema's killer was not Yunosuke but himself; he also said that it was he who had taken her body to the temple. For an entire night he was cross-examined by skeptical investigators.

The killing was motivated by a burst of rage, he maintained. When he got back to the teahouse that night, she'd been there, waiting for Yunosuke. She came and went so much that he couldn't read or study, and it really got on his nerves. He yelled at her, told her to "Fuck off!" but she wouldn't leave. She said that since she was pregnant with Yunosuke's child, if anyone left it should be him, Wataru, not her. He told the police his own family situation was so bad that he had no intention of ever going back to live at home. The teahouse in Kitayama was all he had. The thought of her indifference to anyone's needs but her own made him wild with anger. He lost control, and when he came to himself, he realized he had strangled her. He repeated this story over and over.

Why then was it Yunosuke's sneakers that had left the footprints in the snow? Because he'd worn his friend's shoes to move the body, he insisted. In the end, chiefly because Wataru was at my aunt's house at the time of the crime and couldn't possibly have made it back across town anywhere near the estimated time of death – and because Yunosuke had no alibi of his own – the police concluded that Wataru's story was a fabrication. From then on they treated him as a college kid on the verge of a nervous breakdown.

Yunosuke, meanwhile, stated for the record that he had no idea why his roommate should go to such absurd lengths to protect him. Along with providing vivid details that only someone intimately involved with the murder could have known, he maintained that

Wataru had no connection whatever to the events of that night; that by the time he got back, he, Yunosuke, had already killed Ema and carted off her body, and was packing his bag to leave. When the case came to light, he was roaming around Iwate prefecture all by himself, and where Wataru had been then, he had no idea. The guy was hypersensitive; maybe the news of Ema's death had pushed him over the edge. He had a history of overreacting to people's deaths, anyway. This was Yunosuke's take on it.

Yunosuke's own motive was readily credible. With his life just starting to take off, his girlfriend goes and gets herself pregnant. She won't hear of an abortion, insists he's got to marry her. He has his future to think of and doesn't want to be a father at all, much less marry her and help raise the kid. She says she's not going anywhere, period. Meanwhile the child in her womb gets bigger and bigger. Murder is his only escape...

Yunosuke acknowledged that the killing was largely planned. On the evening of December 14th, they'd run into his roommate's girlfriend, Kyoko Noma, at a coffee shop called A Cappella. On the spot, he'd secretly made up his mind to do it that night, figuring that as long as the other two were together, he would have free use of the teahouse. Wataru wouldn't be back 'til seven thirty at the earliest, which left plenty of time to kill Ema and hide the body.

But when he and Ema were alone in the teahouse, she gave him no chance to attack, and he started to panic. Whenever he got behind her, she would turn to face him. He felt no pity for her. By then she was nothing in his eyes but an object. Finally, as she sat at the *kotatsu*, he pinioned her arms from behind and strangled her. It was then just after eight. He worried briefly about Wataru walking in on him, but his mood was defiant, not afraid; he just wanted to avoid any further complications.

He didn't take her body to the temple to hide it. It had seemed only proper to lay a dead body flat on the earth. That was the sole reason. He carried the body over on his back. It had been extremely heavy. Fortunately he didn't run into anyone on the way.

By the time his roommate came home, the body was safely disposed of. Saying only that he had to take a sudden trip, he packed his things and headed for the station. He knew he would be found out eventually, and intended all along to turn himself in, but he wanted two or three days of freedom first. Rather than guilt, he'd felt a sense of liberation.

The countryside in Iwate, where he wandered around for what he assumed were his last free days on earth, had been beautiful. He'd never in all his days felt so close to nature or so free. He finished by saying, "I'm a fool who killed someone for no good reason, but in the end I don't think what I did was all that strange. I became a killer for the sake of two days of perfect freedom. Compared with fools who kill themselves day in and day out for the sake of money, duty, or reputation, maybe I'm the smart one after all."

Part of his confession was conveyed to the media in rather sensational form, and one weekly magazine ran a sneering article about the crime committed by the son of a wealthy Tokyo hospital director, under the headline "*Après-guerre* Youth Kills Sweetheart for Two Days of Freedom."

Treated like a nutcase by the police and shown the door, Wataru went to stay with his family at Sengendo. He was not allowed to see Yunosuke. Setsuko worried about him and pestered him with questions, but he wouldn't open up. Early one morning, he left. No one knew where he'd gone.

Setsuko called me nearly every day. I was her only outlet. She begged me to let her know as soon as I heard from him, to share any scrap of information. In her fragile state she came down with a bad cold that hung on and on, but she was stronger mentally and more collected than at any time I'd known her. Never once did she complain or get weepy. What she wanted to know was the real reason why Wataru had tried to protect his friend by confessing to a murder he didn't commit. Clearly she refused to accept the idea that he was out of his mind. Over and over I told her I didn't know, that I couldn't imagine what had been in his head.

I didn't go anywhere, just stayed in and waited for Wataru to call. When my aunt went out on errands, I was so afraid of not hearing the phone ring that I didn't even go to the bathroom. After she retired to her room at night, I would curl up inside the *kotatsu* in the living room. Sometimes in the middle of the night I stared at the phone until it seemed to turn into a giant crow that might soon flap its wings and fly off. But the bird never transmitted Wataru's voice. I thought I would go mad. I probably was a little mad, I just didn't know it.

On December 23rd, in the middle of the night, the call finally came. My aunt had gone to her room. I was sitting in the living room listening to the wall clock tick off the seconds. When the phone rang I flew to answer it, grabbing the receiver on the third ring. There was the click of a coin dropping. After that came a sound like ocean surf.

"Hello?" I said. "Wataru? It's you, isn't it?"

Another coin fell, then another. In between came a faint clicking sound, as if the line had been cut off. A fourth coin had fallen by the time he spoke.

"I forgot my address book," he blurted out. "Yours was the only number I could remember. Kyoko. It's been a while. You okay?"

"Where are you?" My pulse was racing so fast I thought my heart might give out. I gripped the receiver.

"By the sea," he said. His voice was low but steady.

"Where? Tell me. Everyone's worried. Setsuko…"

"I don't care about anyone else. Right now I just want to talk to you."

"Are you someplace far away? You're on a public phone. I can hear how fast the coins are dropping."

"I brought a whole slew of coins. We can't waste time, though. Once these are gone, there isn't anywhere around here to get more."

I said his name again, trying desperately to keep the tears out of my voice. "If you only knew how worried I've been."

There was a short silence. I could hear the surf-like sound again.

"I had to talk to you," he said. "That's why I called."

"I don't want to know anything." I gulped back sobs. Tears were pouring down my cheeks. My nose was dribbling onto my upper lip. I shook my head hard, seeking words for what no words could express.

Then, as if to say I could weep and wail all I liked and it wouldn't matter, he began to talk. "Actually," he said, "I called to tell you that Yunosuke and I planned Ema's murder together."

With a great hiccup, I stopped crying. I could picture him smiling ruefully. "But I wasn't serious. I mean, I never thought he'd do it.

I thought it was all a game, that we were just playing around, but he meant it. I didn't know. Although I have to say, when he walked out of A Cappella with her that afternoon, the thought did cross my mind. I hadn't heard anything about the two of them going anywhere that night."

Coins continued to fall rapidly. "Wait a minute," he said, and loaded another handful in the slot, one by one. I listened in silence. The only thing linking me to him now was this fragile telephone connection. If I wasted time with needless talk and tears, the phone would go on devouring coins, hastening the moment when the link between us would be severed.

He went on. "When they left, I had a bad feeling. I was really scared, in fact. But I told myself nothing that crazy could happen. That's why I walked you home, and when your aunt invited me to stay for dinner, I said yes. Dinner was good. She's a really great lady, friendly and fun to be with. I realized again what a good life you have. And she gave me all that food, which I didn't get to eat. It still bothers me."

I sniffled quietly. Wataru softly cleared his throat.

"When I left you at nine and went home, Yunosuke was there. He was deathly pale, and he was throwing things into a travel bag. I could tell something was wrong. Before I could ask, he came right out and said he'd killed Ema. Then he was gone. For about half an hour I sat there in a daze, unable to think straight. Before I knew it, it was nearly eleven. I realized I'd forgotten to ask him where he was going. I ran out the door and went to the train station. There was no sign of him anywhere. I was so out of it, I don't even remember what train I got on. Some random train. The next morning I was in Aomori Station, in the waiting room. I was nearly broke, so I couldn't go anywhere. I just sat there and thought it all through."

He paused. "Kyoko," he said softly, "I thought about all kinds of things. Myself, Yunosuke, the life he and I chose, then meeting you... I was perfectly clear-headed. I've probably never been so clear-headed in my life. I made up my mind to take the blame for what he did because it was just as much my crime as his. Right? I mean, if it weren't for me, he'd never have done it. There wouldn't have been any need."

"That's why you told that lie?" I asked quietly. "If you wanted to save him, why not tell the police the truth about you and him instead? If they knew his real motive, that might have counted for something."

"No, that wouldn't have saved him. Neither of us could ever have publicly owned up to that, even under duress. If it came to that, we'd both kill ourselves first. That's how it is. There's no getting around it."

"I don't understand," I said. "Why would you…"

"Kyoko," he said, his tone softening. "You don't have to understand. Believe me, a sweet kid like you doesn't need to. But even without understanding, you stood by us. I was sure you wouldn't tell the police, and you didn't. For that I'm grateful."

His politeness saddened me, but I held my tongue.

He let out a sigh. "You were the first girl I ever loved."

I closed my eyes. My lips began to tremble uncontrollably.

"I loved you," he repeated in a low voice. "Really and truly. I think with you I could have changed. I would have, I know it. The time we spent together was great. The sex, too. I was clumsy, I know… I hope you don't mind about that. But I loved making love to you, and I loved you."

A coin dropped. It made a sound like a pebble plopping onto moist sand. I felt myself growing faint.

"I'm so sorry for what happened to Ema." His voice was barely audible now. "She was a good kid. She just kind of grated on his nerves sometimes. If it hadn't been for that I think maybe the four of us could have gone on the way we were, and been pretty happy, despite everything. We could have made it work. Because I loved you, Kyoko, and Yunosuke cared for Ema in his own way. Ah, no more coins. Now we'll be cut off."

"No!" I cried. "I'll call you back. Go somewhere where I can call you! Please, Wataru!"

"Goodbye, Kyoko," he said, his voice too cheerful. "I think knowing you is the best thing that ever happened to me."

I kept calling his name. But the line suddenly went dead, like a stereo when its plug is pulled.

The next morning, his body was found in a room in a small seaside inn on the Noto Peninsula. He had hanged himself from the lintel. At his feet were three letters, one addressed to Setsuko, one to me, and one to Yunosuke. The names were all different, but the message was the same. It consisted of a single brief line: *"Now I can sleep easy. Wataru."*

THE LAST CHAPTER

It was past eleven o'clock by the time the two customers finally got up and left. Setsuko saw them off, and as soon as she came back she began closing up shop. The young part-time worker had been checking her watch, and when Setsuko gave her permission to leave she flew out the door with barely a nod.

"That's the younger generation for you," said Setsuko with a wry smile. "No work ethic. Can't even say a proper hello or goodbye."

I smiled back at her. She invited me to come and sit at the counter, which was lit by a single overhead light. All the other lights were turned off. Glass in hand, I moved across. She made us each another Coke highball and said, "Cheers, again." I echoed softly, "Cheers."

Slowly sipping her drink, Setsuko gave me a long look from behind the counter. Her eyes crinkled with apparent pleasure. Close up, I could see a sprinkling of gray at her temples, but she was still gorgeous. She made me think of a petal encased in ice, fresh despite the passage of time.

"You haven't changed a bit, Kyoko."

"Yes, I have." I laughed and said, "I'll be forty next year."

"Really?"

"It's been twenty years, after all."

"So it has." She nodded, thinking. "Twenty years, imagine that."

"How long have you been working here?"

"Going on eight years. How'd you ever find me, anyway?"

"I called Senmado and asked. It was about ten days ago. They wouldn't give me your home phone, but they did tell me you had a bar in this part of town."

"So that's it," she said, nodding, then added: "I got married."

My face lit up. Hers reddened slightly.

"He used to work managing a snack bar near the university. He changed careers, and now runs a secondhand bookstore. The owner of the snack bar rents this place to me. So you could say I'm following in my husband's footsteps."

"It's a nice place."

"I don't know. One thing it's not is lucrative. It's more of a hobby than a job. I haven't got much business sense – customers don't exactly flock in."

"How are your step-parents?"

"He died last year. She's fine, but we're virtual strangers. I almost never see her."

"Do you have any children?"

"Two, a year apart. A boy in the first year of high school and a girl finishing junior high. She reminds me a little of you in the old days, Kyoko."

"Tough cookie, huh?"

"No," she said with a laugh, slowly shaking her head. "She's sweet and sincere. I tell myself that one of these days she'll fall in love with someone like Wataru. I hope so."

She turned around and put on a CD. Strains of Diana Ross and the Supremes singing "Love Child" filled the air. We listened for a while. A crack opened in time and space, and a narrow stream filled slowly with water, bearing us back to the past.

"Are you married, Kyoko?" she asked, looking up.

I nodded. "I stayed single 'til I was thirty. My husband is a psychiatric doctor. I work as a psychotherapist in the same hospital, mainly treating patients with psychosomatic problems. New college students, mostly, and people with new jobs."

I didn't tell Setsuko why I'd chosen that career. Two decades ago I'd failed the entrance exams, as might be expected after those shocking events, so I left my aunt's house and went back to Tokyo to live with my parents. It wasn't 'til a year later that I finally got accepted into college and began to study psychology. What motivated me to keep on in the field and become a psychotherapist was the impact of my relationship with Wataru. I became interested in everything to do with the human mind, to the point where nothing else seemed to matter as much.

"You always were different," said Setsuko, nodding thoughtfully, with a refined smile on her lips that I remembered well. "What else? Children?"

"One boy." I placed a cigarette in my mouth, and Setsuko lit it for me with a lighter. "He's still only seven, so I left him with my parents today. Poor kid – with both parents working, he doesn't get much attention. He's probably screwed up already."

"Did your work bring you to Sendai?"

"No." I leaned an elbow on the counter, my cigarette propped between two fingers, and looked her square in the face. "I came to see you."

She frowned slightly, taking this to heart.

"I came to see you, Setsuko," I repeated slowly. "I wanted to come back to Sendai, to go back to A Cappella. I've wanted to come for twenty years, but I never had the courage. I'm such a wimp. If I'd come when I was younger, I'd probably have stood in the middle of the street and bawled my eyes out."

"Not now?"

"Like I said, I'll be forty next year." I averted my eyes, which were starting to mist over, and took a deep drag on my cigarette. "Even if I wanted to cry, there's no way I'd do it in the middle of the street."

Setsuko laughed softly. She put some ice cubes in her glass, filled it with whiskey and took a sip. "I often wonder what would have happened if Wataru had lived… and married you. Remember what I said one time? That you two should get out, rent an apartment and start living together."

"I remember," I said.

"You meant so much to him. He talked about his feelings for you all the time. I think you'd have been happy together. Some little thing made it all fall apart, didn't it? He was so sensitive. So was I, for that matter, but not nearly as much as he was. He didn't have to go and die, though. Something good is bound to happen if you stick it out. Look at me. I used to be an emotional wreck. I'm living proof."

I nodded, remembering her suicide attempt over the failed romance with Araki. She lightly licked her lips and looked at me.

"You know something, Kyoko?" she said. "There's one thing I still don't understand. Why *did* he die?"

The ominous thudding of my heart that I thought I'd forgotten came back. Taking care not to betray any emotion or change my expression, I shook my head as slowly as I could. "I've no idea."

"No, of course not," she said with a sigh. "Nobody else can ever know the real reason why someone kills himself, I suppose."

Little by little, I let my breath out. A long-suppressed surge of nausea came rising up. I felt the way a dormant volcano must feel when something happens to set it off, just before a spew of magma shoots up into the air.

Beyond any doubt, the responsibility for Ema's death – the responsibility for driving Yunosuke to kill her – lay in no small measure with me. And responsibility for driving Wataru to suicide was mine as well. Now was the time to own up and make a clean breast of it all.

Again I asked myself why I'd come to Sendai. Not just to wallow in sentimentality, surely; that I could do anytime, anywhere. Listening to the Rolling Stones or Bach was all it ever took to whisk me back in time. Then what was the real reason for my decision to come here and track Setsuko down and see her in person? Wasn't it a release I was looking for? *The statute of limitations has run out by now; now I can let her in on the secret…* Hadn't this thought been in the back of my mind?

Just as I opened my mouth to speak, she beat me to it. "As a matter of fact…" she began. If she hadn't spoken then, I think I would have told her everything. And so I lost my chance to confess, for good.

"…Yunosuke was paroled five years ago." She said it without emotion, in the same tone a person might use to speak of a brother just back from a trip abroad. "He was a model prisoner, and his sentence got drastically reduced. For a while he was living alone in Tokyo, working in a factory, but now he's in Okinawa. Last year, I think it was, he sent me a postcard saying he got married. His wife is Okinawan, with kids from a first marriage. Just like that, he became the father of three. They run a souvenir store, he said. He asked me to come down for a visit."

"So in all those years… you never…?"

"No, I never saw him once. But from time to time I'd write to him. He wrote back, too. All either of us said was things we remembered about Wataru. I'd like to go see him, I really would. But I don't know, maybe it would be better not to. I do know how to reach him, though, so if... if you wanted to get in touch with him, Kyoko, I could help. What do you want to do?"

I gave her a vague smile, but didn't ask for the information. If Yunosuke had rubbed out the past and embarked on a new and happier life, I could only wish him well.

I decided to say nothing. No need to dredge up the past. If I kept my mouth shut, the rest of Setsuko's life would probably run its peaceful course. She would age gracefully, meddling in her children's studies and romances, quarrelling with her husband, experiencing the ordinary joys of marriage and motherhood. In another ten or fifteen years, some sunny day she would pose for the camera with her grandchild in her arms, a beaming grandmother. Telling someone with all that ahead of her the facts of the past, simply because they were the facts, was more than I had the courage to do.

Even the most tragic events gradually fade in time. Memories, if left alone, eventually change their coloration. Setsuko had successfully overcome the events of the past as she understood them. What she needed from me now was not to unearth them, but simply to affirm a different, altered past, one she could remember without pain.

It would be wrong to say anything, I reminded myself strongly. In so doing I confirmed that for a time, Wataru and I had been closer than any other two people. I found a bleak pleasure in the thought.

"How long are you in town for?" asked Setsuko.

"I'm leaving tomorrow afternoon."

"Won't you drop by the house before you go, if you have time? I'd like you to meet my husband."

"Thanks," I said, "but I'm afraid I won't have time. I want to visit the cemetery."

"You mean... Wataru's grave?"

"His and Ema's."

"Yes, of course," she said with a wan smile. "I always light some incense at her grave at the equinox."

"I bet she's mad as hell at me," I said. "I haven't been to her grave once in all these years. And besides..."

"What?"

"Nothing," I lied, and brought my glass to my lips. My eyes stung with tears. *Ema. Ema.* It was such a long time since I'd said her name to anyone. She was a victim, certainly, but at the same time she'd played a leading part in the whole tale. Without her our saga would never have begun, and without her it would never have ended. She'd always been at the heart of our slight, mysterious story, someone whose role drove the action rapidly to its end.

Resting her cheek on one hand, Setsuko said, "If Ema were alive, she'd be turning forty next year, too. I can just picture it. She'd be a jolly, kindhearted wife with a big family."

"You never know," I said. "She might just as easily be an international businesswoman, zipping around the world. Or a social activist, the kind who runs for office and wins by a landslide."

Setsuko laughed. For a while after that we sipped our drinks, misty-eyed, and talked some more about Ema and about ourselves. The night wore on, yet time continued to flow ever backwards into the past.

I remembered my aunt, and her little dog Mogu. The winter of my sophomore year in college, she'd met and married a widower who was a violinist, and moved with him to Osaka. Mogu went along. The marriage was happy, I heard, but one winter's day two years later she died of heart failure. Mogu followed her in the summer, dying of old age.

Shortly after two in the morning, I stood up to go. I attempted to pay the bill, but Setsuko wouldn't hear of it. I thanked her and headed for the door.

"Forgot to ask," I said, and turned back. "Is A Cappella the same?"

"Hardly," she said, with a half smile. "It's long gone. It's been out of business nearly ten years now."

"The building's gone too?"

"Without a trace. There's some brand-new building there now. You'd never know it was the same place."

"I see," I said, nodding. "Well, everything changes."

"Yes, but I was sort of glad to see it go. You know what I mean? If it were still there, just the way it used to be, going inside would be heartbreaking."

We were standing facing each other by the door.

"I'm glad you came," she said.

"Me too," I replied.

Her lips quivered, and she looked on the verge of tears, but she stayed dry-eyed. We smiled and shook hands. Her hand was cool and moist.

Outside, the street was still bustling. Making my way past bar hostesses shoving drunken customers into taxis, I went to the corner, turned again in front of Fujisaki Department Store, and entered the arcade. It was almost empty. My footsteps echoed loudly.

I spied the sign for Sakharov, the cake shop where on the night of the Star Festival the four of us had eaten porcupine cakes. The shop's exterior had been extensively refinished but the atmosphere was the same. I stopped in front of it, took a deep breath, and stood looking in with my mouth half open like a drunk in a trance. A trio of college-aged men passed by, all of them drunk and staggering. The one on the right looked a little like Wataru, I thought, but it might have been my imagination.

I walked on. Turned left at the next corner. Went on another fifty yards, then retraced my steps. The building where A Cappella used to be,, that old three-storey dirty beige building, was nowhere to be seen. In its place stood a big new complex of fashionable boutiques.

I went up to the entrance and peered in. Narrow stairs leading down to the basement floor also looked new, but they seemed to me to be about where the old ones had been. Below was a combined tearoom and restaurant.

I went across the street, leaned against the shutter of a closed boutique and smoked a cigarette. Beyond the swirl of smoke a vision arose. At any moment the door to A Cappella would open, and trooping up the grubby, odorous steps would come the whole gang, with Reiko and Juri not far behind. I closed my eyes and banished the unfamiliar building now standing before me. Behind my eyelids rose an old, monochromatic world. A world where A Cappella was its old self again.

It all came flooding back: the well-remembered smells of cheap coffee and cigarettes; the strains of Bach's Brandenburg Concertos and Pachelbel's Canon. In one corner I sat, looking out of sorts. I was scribbling intently into an open notebook, wearing my chocolate-brown jacket and lace-up boots. I had a cigarette between my lips, and just as I lit it, the door opened and in came Ema, Yunosuke, and Wataru. I turned and smiled at them. Wataru looked Jewish, the way he always did. He came and sat next to me. The Canon started up. "Kyoko," he said. I looked at him, my heart pounding. "Kyoko…"

I came to myself and opened my eyes. A cold, dry autumn wind blew past, and there was a slight ringing in my ears. In the distance I saw a haze of wet-looking neon signs. Wataru was gone. Ema and Yunosuke too, and the café called A Cappella – all of it was gone.

I stood there until I finished my cigarette, then stubbed it out on the pavement and took a deep breath. After a final glance at the building, now nothing but a big square box, I walked off toward my hotel.

Of all my old friends, the only one I've stayed in touch with is Juri. A year after high school she passed the exam to get into a fine arts university in Tokyo, and just after graduating she married an aspiring artist two years her senior. They live in a Tokyo suburb, and she does a little painting of her own, but mostly helps arrange exhibitions of her husband's work. We get together about once a year. We usually go out for a drink or two. For health reasons she doesn't drink much anymore, but she still smokes as much as ever. We don't talk much about the past. Our conversation mostly revolves around housing loans, golf, art, health, our pets – simple things like that.

It doesn't happen very often, but once in a while we'll slip into a reminiscence. When Reiko's name comes up, we always wonder where she is and what she's doing now. To this day, Juri calls her "reptilian" and does imitations of her expression. It always cracks me up. After I laugh, my eyes fill with tears. But I've never wept openly in front of her.